RUNAWAY
BRIDE

RUNAWAY BRIDE

·

Marilyn Shank

AVALON BOOKS
NEW YORK

PRINTED IN THE UNITED STATES OF AMERICA
ON ACID-FREE PAPER
BY HADDON CRAFTSMEN, BLOOMSBURG, PENNSYLVANIA

To my husband John, who saw the vision,
and my dear critique buddies, who kept me on task.

Prologue

"Hurry up, Hannah! The photographer's ready to start taking pictures!"

As her fiancé's voice boomed through the dressing room door, the anxiety Hannah had been experiencing all afternoon increased. "I'll be right there, Paul," she promised, trying to suppress her mounting panic.

She turned to face her mother. "Suddenly I'm not so sure about this wedding, Mom. Am I supposed to feel this nervous?"

"Of course, dear. You're a bride. It comes with the territory."

Hannah checked her image in the full-length mirror. The satin princess-style gown with its bodice of Chantilly lace made her look like a perfect bride. So why didn't she feel like one?

1

As she and her mother made their way through the narrow hallway and into the sanctuary, Hannah's uneasiness grew. The photographer, ready to take pre-wedding portraits, smiled with approval. "Here's the bride now, and she's a beauty!"

Hannah forced a smile. "Thank you."

Paul strode toward her and took hold of her arm. "It's about time. You've kept the photographer waiting."

As she met his gaze, Hannah sensed her fiancé's disapproval. Paul didn't comment on her gown or say she made a lovely bride. The photographer seemed more interested in Hannah's appearance than her prospective husband.

Paul ushered Hannah up the carpeted aisle of the sanctuary. She felt more like a disobedient child who'd run away from her father at the shopping mall, than a woman about to be married.

She spotted her father sitting stiffly in the second pew. While their relationship had never been close, she was glad he'd come for the wedding. Pulling away from Paul, she spoke to her father. "Thanks for coming, Daddy."

He nodded. "It's hard to believe you're all grown up. I . . . I hope you'll be happy."

It was as emotional a statement as he'd ever made and Hannah considered giving him a hug but thought better of it. Hugging didn't fall within her father's comfort zone. "Thanks, Daddy," she said quietly.

"Hannah? The man is waiting."

Obediently, Hannah took her place beside Paul on the rostrum where golden candelabras and lacy ferns created a romantic setting. She'd chosen the Chapel of the Pines for their private ceremony because the little church was intimate and peaceful—a good place for a husband and wife to exchange their wedding vows.

As she and Paul stood side by side, Hannah felt one step removed from reality. She managed to pose and smile in accordance with the photographer's instructions, but her thoughts drifted back to childhood. Scenes flashed through her mind like reruns of home movies. In each one, her father ruled their family with an iron hand. And her mother moved quietly in his shadow.

"Just one more shot of the happy couple. Then we'll ask the bride's parents to pose for a picture," the photographer said.

The panic inside Hannah suddenly escalated to unmanageable proportions. In an instant, the truth hit her with incredible force. *Paul is just like Daddy!* Why hadn't she seen it sooner?

She couldn't marry Paul Arnold! He was a control freak, like her father. She glanced at her mother who sat demurely beside her father. This dear lady had spent her entire life carrying out her husband's instructions.

"Stop," Hannah said firmly, glancing at the photographer. "No more pictures."

Paul turned to glare at her. It wasn't the kind of look a groom ought to give his bride on their wedding day. "Don't tell the man his business," Paul snapped. "Say, what's gotten into you, anyway?"

Hannah's panic suddenly subsided and she felt surprisingly calm as she turned to face her fiancé. "I'm sorry, Paul, but I can't marry you. It would be a mistake for both of us."

A look of rage flashed across Paul's face. "What in the . . ."

"Our marriage would never work. I should have realized it long ago."

His fiery gaze made Hannah certain she'd made the right choice. She leaned forward and planted a gentle kiss on Paul's cheek, and, feeling better already, turned and walked down the center aisle of the Chapel of the Pines.

Alone.

Chapter One

Hannah lifted the heavy satin skirt of her wedding gown and left the Chapel of the Pines, realizing that her carefully planned life had just come to a screeching halt. If she didn't want to marry Paul Arnold, what *did* she want?

Anonymity and lots of it. And a change. A big change. Climbing into her red Mustang convertible, gown and all, Hannah headed for oblivion.

Knowing only that she had to get away from Kansas City, she drove south on Highway 71. She didn't take time to remove her veil and after it blew in her face several times, obstructing her view, she pulled out the clips and stuffed it into her overnight bag on the floor of the front seat. At midnight, she crossed from Missouri into Arkansas, trying to forget that she and Paul had tickets on a red-eye flight to Honolulu.

She drove a while longer, then spotted a sign for Willa Mae's Diner just ahead. Because she hadn't eaten since noon the day before, Hannah pulled into the diner's parking lot. Gathering up fistfuls of wedding gown, she hurried inside, ignoring curious stares from several truck drivers.

Men. Every one she'd ever gotten close to had been controlling and manipulative. Her father, the king of domination, had nearly ruined her life. And she'd almost given Paul Arnold the same opportunity.

She slid into a booth, further wrinkling the gown that the seamstress had pressed so carefully in preparation for the ceremony. A plump, gray-haired woman, whose name badge read WILLA MAE, poured Hannah a steaming cup of coffee. ''What can I bring you, hon?''

''The biggest plate of biscuits and gravy you have. My diet's history.''

The waitress nodded. ''You've got it.''

Willa Mae served the biscuits on a platter instead of a luncheon plate. She leaned toward Hannah. ''I don't want to pry, but if you need somethin' besides breakfast, let me know.''

Hannah smiled feebly. ''Thanks.''

After downing the high-fat meal, Hannah began to wilt. She felt as if she could slip right off the booth, dissolve into a heap of white satin, and sleep forever.

She reached for her purse and was disappointed to find her billfold contained only twenty dollars. She and Paul had pooled their funds and put all their traveler's checks into his name. What a fool she'd been.

After paying the bill, only fourteen dollars and ninety-six cents and a Gold Card stood between Hannah and starvation. Hunger and homelessness were two conditions she hadn't planned on encountering this summer.

Willa Mae came over and handed her a key. "You look like you could use some rest. I own the cabins behind the diner, and number four is vacant. Go and sleep it off."

"Thank you," Hannah said, too tired to object. She dragged herself and the yards of rumpled satin through the dusty red Arkansas soil, unlocked cabin number four, and dropped, exhausted, onto the bed.

The next thing Hannah knew, someone was gently shaking her shoulder. Willa Mae stood over her with a tray of food that made the biscuits and gravy look like an appetizer. "It's almost noon. I thought you might be getting hungry."

Hannah sat up and took the tray. "Thanks. You've been so nice."

"Anything else you need, honey?"

Hannah sighed. "Yes. I need a job."

"Summer's a good time to get work around here.

Lots of resorts and camps need staff. I'll bring you the want ads.''

Willa Mae returned with the newspaper, then went back to the diner. As Hannah scanned the ads, one caught her attention:

Wanted Immediately: An Activities Director for Camp Wildwood. Apply at Pine Bluff Lodge. Ask for Jacob Reynolds, Camp Director.

After lunch, Hannah grabbed her suitcase from the Mustang's trunk, showered, then dug through her clothes for an outfit befitting a job interview. Rifling through the swimsuits and nightgowns she'd purchased for her honeymoon, she finally chose white slacks and a flowered silk blouse. She sighed. She'd intended to wear this outfit on Waikiki Beach as she and Paul walked barefoot in the sand.

She smeared extra foundation on the bags under her eyes that rivaled her suitcase in size, and finally added a pair of sunglasses for camouflage. Then she carried her dishes back to the diner. ''What do I owe you for the cabin?'' she asked Willa Mae, wondering what she'd do if the bill exceeded fourteen dollars and ninety-six cents.

The proprietress patted Hannah's hand. ''Consider it a non-wedding present.''

''I can't do that. Here. Take my credit card.''

Willa Mae shook her head. She probably realized

Hannah was dead broke. Or else she thought that any woman running around alone in a wedding gown was a mental case and she'd better not upset her.

"Thanks. I'll pay back every cent," Hannah promised. "As soon as I find a job."

"Did you see anything in the paper?"

Hannah pointed to the ad she'd circled. "This one sounds promising."

"Camp Wildwood's not far from here. It's a pretty decent facility, but the kids can be a handful."

"I can't afford to be choosy. Where is Camp Wildwood?"

As Willa Mae rattled off directions, Hannah scribbled them into the margins of the newspaper. Then she leaned over the counter and gave the proprietress an affectionate squeeze. "Thanks for everything, Willa Mae. You're an angel."

The older woman smiled. "I'm here if you need me. By the way, what's your name?"

"Hannah. Hannah Hastings."

Relief flooded over Hannah as she realized that her last name was still Hastings. She'd come frighteningly close to changing it to Arnold—a step that would certainly have ruined her life.

After stuffing her wedding gown and suitcase into the Mustang's trunk, she headed for Camp Wildwood. Willa Mae's directions took her over a gravel road that wound far back into the Arkansas hills. After several miles of dusty driving, Hannah spotted the sign for

Pine Bluff Lodge. She parked her Mustang and entered the building where a young woman in cutoffs and a tank top approached her. Obviously a bodybuilder, the woman had muscles most men would envy. She shot Hannah a skeptical glance. "Are you lost? Looks like you're headed for a tropical island."

Hannah ignored the crack and held up the ad. "I'm here to talk with Mr. Reynolds about the Activities Director position."

The young woman eyed her dubiously. "Honey, some of our sixth graders are twice your size. Why, they'd make mincemeat out of you in—"

"May I be of service?"

A resonant male voice behind them cut into the conversation. "I'm Jacob Reynolds."

Hannah turned to face a tall, very attractive man with jet black hair and deep brown eyes. His well-proportioned body had been bronzed by the sun. "I've come about your ad, Mr. Reynolds," she finally said. "I'm Hannah Hastings."

He hesitated a moment, making Hannah wonder if he, too, thought the sixth graders would make mincemeat out of her.

Then he said, "Right this way, please." So she followed him to a small office.

Even with her recent vow to eternal singleness, Jacob Reynolds captured Hannah's attention. He wore a T-shirt with the Camp Wildwood logo, jean shorts, and a pair of Nikes. Hannah took a deep breath and reminded herself that she was finished with men. She'd made that decision on the long drive from Kansas City.

Mr. Reynolds took a seat behind a black metal desk and gestured to a folding chair across from him. "Please sit down, Miss Hastings."

"Thank you."

He surveyed her with interest. "Have you worked as an Activities Director before?"

"Well, not exactly."

He quirked an eyebrow. "How close did you come?"

Hannah cleared her throat. "I attended camp once. Well, it was actually a day camp."

He frowned. "So you have no experience."

"I'm a schoolteacher. I have lots of experience."

"What grade do you teach?"

"Kindergarten."

His brow furrowed slightly. "Miss Hastings, this camp is for inner-city kids, most of them ornery, and all of them dedicated to making life miserable for camp personnel. I doubt that teaching kindergarten is adequate preparation."

"Teaching kindergarten isn't a cushy job, Mr. Reynolds, and my students are not little angels. Last year, a skunk that Julie Browning brought for show-and-tell got loose in our classroom. Julie said the animal had been de-scented, but that wasn't the case. And Ben Anderson's pet snake slithered down the hall to the music room, scaring the fourth graders half to death. So you see, I handle difficult situations every day. And,'' she added hastily, ''I'm not unfamiliar with wildlife.''

As Jake studied the woman across from him, he reminded himself to stay objective. But he found himself distracted by her exceptional good looks. Miss Hastings's creamy skin was flawless, except for a trail of freckles that marched over the bridge of her nose. Her blond hair looked windblown and tousled and the designer sunglasses she'd taken off moments earlier revealed fascinating blue eyes. She smelled like gardenias—an aroma incongruous to the Arkansas woods.

He shook off the momentary attraction. This woman wasn't suited to camp life. The silk blouse and white slacks she wore would be perfect for a Caribbean cruise, but they wouldn't last five minutes on a campground. The lovely lady belonged on a brochure advertising exotic vacation spots. Not at Camp Wildwood.

''My activities director broke her leg and I need to replace her,'' Jake explained. ''I'm looking for someone who can take the kids horseback riding and on canoe trips—someone who'll teach wildlife classes and lead nature hikes. I'm sorry, Miss Hastings, but I don't think . . .''

The woman stood and pulled herself to her full height—five-foot-three, tops. Her stunning blue eyes were fired with determination. "Mr. Reynolds, I can do this job if you'll give me a chance. I ride horses, I've taken float trips, and I love nature. I've studied basket weaving and I'm an experienced teacher. Surely those are credentials enough."

He sighed. No one else had applied for the position, and camp started tomorrow. If he didn't hire Miss Hastings, he'd have to teach the classes and conduct the field trips himself, and he had far too much to do already. "All right," he said reluctantly. "You're hired."

Her delectable eyes softened and she smiled a captivating smile. "Really? That's great."

"You might not think so after you hear what it pays."

But the lady didn't flinch when he quoted the salary, didn't recoil when he told her she'd be spending the summer in a cabin without air-conditioning. She didn't even wince when he pointed out that the mosquitoes were gargantuan and that water moccasins flocked to Camp Wildwood almost as freely as the campers. She nodded agreeably and seemed perfectly content.

This job may be short-lived, Hannah thought dismally. *I'll probably be carried off by a family of water moccasins on my first night at camp.*

To be honest, which she hadn't been with Mr. Reynolds, she hated anything that crawled. She couldn't distinguish one spider from another, and she was hopelessly addicted to air-conditioning. Why had she felt compelled to secure this position at Camp Nightmare?

Then she remembered. She had no place to live, one suitcase of inappropriate clothing, and fourteen dollars and ninety-six cents. "Is my board included in the benefit package?"

He nodded. "Three squares a day. We have a full-time cook who you may need to assist occasionally." He studied her carefully. "You *can* cook?"

Kids ate hot dogs and pizza. That couldn't be too difficult. "Sure," she fibbed. "I can cook."

When Jacob Reynolds smiled approvingly, Hannah felt a little guilty about the way she'd slanted the truth. The horse she'd ridden was actually a Shetland pony. She had floated down a river once—in a rowboat. And the basket she'd woven didn't look anything like the pattern and kept toppling over.

But she'd learn. She'd do whatever was required to become the best activities director Camp Wildwood ever had.

Hannah suddenly remembered she was far from civilization. "I don't suppose there's a library nearby?"

"You won't have much time to read, Miss Hastings. We'll keep you pretty busy."

"I wanted to brush up on wildflowers and trees for the nature walks."

Mr. Reynolds pointed to a shelf that contained a couple dozen ancient volumes, layered with dust. "Those will help. Feel free to borrow them."

"Thanks."

"I'll walk you to your cabin and show you where to park. We don't drive on the grounds. It spoils our man-in-tune-with-nature philosophy."

As Hannah followed the broad-shouldered camp director out of the lodge and into the sultry Arkansas afternoon, she wondered if she'd made a mistake by landing this job. The last thing she needed was daily contact with a terrific-looking man.

Discipline, Hannah, she chided herself. *Set a goal and work toward it.* Her goal was to be an independent woman and she'd stick to that goal at all costs. But it would help if her new employer was over forty with a potbelly.

Suddenly, a green creature with incredibly long legs sailed through the air and landed on the neckline of Hannah's blouse. Turning away, she tried desperately to brush off the nasty thing, but it clung to her for dear life.

"What's wrong?" Mr. Reynolds asked.

"I . . . I think it bit me!"

"What bit you? A spider?"

"I don't know what it is. I can't see it very well."

"Turn around."

Reluctantly, she turned to face him.

"It's only a grasshopper. It can't possibly hurt you."

Oh, no? At that moment, the awful thing crept up

her neck and began performing sadistic somersaults against her skin.

"Oh, get it, get it!" she pleaded.

Mr. Reynolds came closer. "Hold still, Miss Hastings. Wait . . . wait . . . There. I've got him."

After what seemed an eternity, Mr. Reynolds grasped the creature and tossed it into the bushes.

Hannah took a steadying breath. "Thanks."

"No problem."

While he'd been polite about the incident, Hannah knew what the camp director must be thinking. How on earth could a woman teach nature classes and take students on hikes into the woods if a single grasshopper sent her into a frenzy?

She hadn't figured that out herself.

They continued walking until they reached a cluster of log cabins that looked like children's playhouses. Mr. Reynolds stopped at the first cabin and pushed open the door for her to enter. "This is your new home."

They entered and Hannah gazed around the tiny, one-room structure. It was unbearably hot and the musty smell was stifling. "This is, um, very nice," she said, lying through her teeth.

Two broken-down bunk beds, a pair of aqua upholstered kitchen chairs straight from the fifties, a mirror with most of the paint chipped off its wooden frame, and a small round table made up the furnishings. One naked light bulb dangled from the ceiling.

Hannah tried to remain calm. "Where's the bathroom?"

"About a block away. We have a community bathhouse that the female campers and staff all share." He eyed her skeptically. "Can you manage?"

"Of course, I can manage," Hannah declared. But the thought of actually living in this minuscule, overheated closet made her slightly nauseated.

The only way she could survive here would be to fix the place up. That thought encouraged her. "I didn't bring any bedding or towels, Mr. Reynolds, since I wasn't certain I'd get the job."

"Call me Jake," he said. "There's a general store ten miles from here in a little town called Sunset Bay. Since our first staff meeting doesn't start until nine P.M., you'll have plenty of time for shopping."

Shopping! He'd finally mentioned an activity Hannah excelled at.

"Great! Would you give me directions to Sunset Bay?"

"I need to pick up some supplies myself. You can ride along, if you like. Meet me at the lodge in half an hour."

"Fine. And thanks for everything, Mr. Reynolds."

"Jake."

The grin he shot her made Hannah's pulse skitter. The only way she could possibly make this job work was to keep her mind on her work and off of the appealing camp director.

After Jake left, Hannah sat down on one of her kitchen chairs and surveyed the small structure that would serve as her summer home. It looked pathetic. Everything in the place was a dirty brown—the walls, the floor, the table, and the bunk beds. Her aqua chairs added the only spark of color. Besides being ugly, the cabin was also filthy. Cobwebs clung to the rafters while mouse droppings and dead bugs littered the floor.

But she'd better look on the bright side. At least she wasn't homeless anymore. She noticed a ragged old broom beside the door and set to work.

After sweeping away the surface dirt, she moved the bunks together, creating a double canopy bed of sorts. Then she arranged her table and chairs under a window. It would take some doing to make this place livable. But she'd make it cozy if it killed her.

Later, when she walked up the hill to the lodge, Hannah felt almost happy. She'd probably overreacted to her new employer's good looks. After all, she'd been stressed from the trauma of canceling the wedding. And sleep deprived, as well.

She opened the screen door to the lodge and saw Jake talking with the bodybuilder. When he looked up at her and smiled, Hannah felt the same spark of pleasure.

He came toward her. "Are you ready, Hannah?"

"I'm ready."

He touched her arm casually, steering her toward

the door and her heart was off and running. She'd better get some sleep fast and get her body back on track. She wasn't used to runaway emotions and did not intend to indulge them. For the first time in her life she was an independent woman. And she planned to stay that way.

She and Jake set out for Sunset Bay in his Bronco and when they arrived at the general store, they grabbed carts and went in opposite directions. While short of cash, at least she'd brought along a credit card.

When Hannah finished shopping, she met Jake at the front of the store. "Did you find everything?" he asked.

"Yes, thanks."

Jake's mouth dropped open as his new activities director began unloading her cart. Pastel sheets, a lace-edged comforter with a matching pillow sham, a good-sized area rug, and two pair of ruffled curtains. "We don't usually aim for the Good Housekeeping Seal of Approval, Hannah. These are cabins, not model homes."

She smiled pleasantly. "My surroundings mean a lot to me. I know camp life is rugged. But at the end of the day, I like to come home to a cheerful atmosphere."

You've really botched it this time, Jake told himself. He'd hired Susie Homemaker and put her in charge of a bunch of roughneck kids. Before he could get thoroughly depressed over that fact, she laid out more of her purchases. "Mousetraps and blue spray paint?" he asked. "Do you plan to spray the mice blue and give them a nice funeral?"

Hannah's generous mouth curved into a lovely smile. "No, silly. The spray paint is for the frame on my mirror. It's badly chipped."

While Jake couldn't fathom what she was planning to do to that poor cabin, he couldn't deny that Hannah fascinated him. The more he tried to fight off the attraction, the stronger it became.

Her final purchases were more appropriate. Bug spray, a flashlight, and a flyswatter. When all the selections were heaped onto the counter, the cashier rang up the total.

"Ninety-five dollars and fourteen cents," the woman announced.

Hannah slipped a Visa Gold Card from her billfold and handed it to the cashier, who handed it right back. "Sorry, ma'am. We don't accept credit cards."

Hannah's mouth dropped open. "But I don't have enough cash." She turned to Jake. "This is just awful. I can't live in that cabin the way it looks now."

Jake stared at the pile of frilly linens that had no earthly function in the Arkansas Ozarks. As the camp director, he'd run into some pretty strange situations, and while he prided himself on his problem-solving skills, he'd never come up against anyone like Hannah Hastings.

Rather than have her drag all the items back and reshelve them, Jake whipped out his billfold, peeled off five crisp twenty-dollar bills, and slapped them onto the counter. "This will cover it," he told the cashier.

Hannah shook her head, sending her silky blond hair dancing around her shoulders. "No, Jake. I won't take your money. I'll just put these things back."

She crammed the comforter into the cart and was reaching for the ruffled curtains when he caught her wrist. When her enticing blue eyes met his, Jake swallowed hard, surprised by the emotions this zany lady stirred inside him.

"You aren't taking my money. It's just a loan. I'll deduct the amount from your first paycheck."

"Oh." She glanced down at his hand, which still gripped her wrist, then back into his eyes. "I suppose that's acceptable."

Jake found himself drowning in the scent of gardenias. He quickly turned Hannah loose and took a giant step back, determined to clear his head.

He'd have to watch out for the power harnessed in this woman's eyes. They were the color of a summer sky. And they touched a place deep inside Jake he didn't want disturbed.

The cashier took his money and handed him the change. "Thank you, sir."

"Yes, thank you," Hannah echoed.

As Jake helped carry her purchases out of the store,

he wondered if it was too late to fire Hannah. He could tell her that he refused to have his cabins converted into dollhouses and that he couldn't have his staff smelling like gardenias.

But he didn't say either of those things. As she climbed into his Bronco, filling it with the fragrance of a tropical paradise, Jake realized that one way or another he'd have to make this arrangement work. The campers would arrive early tomorrow morning. And, like it or not, Hannah was the only activities director he had.

Chapter Two

Jake kept his eyes riveted on the highway as they drove back toward camp. Hannah felt certain he was annoyed about their shopping trip. "What kind of work do you do when you're not directing camps?" she asked, hoping to pull him out of his reverie.

"I'm an attorney. I practice in Kansas City."

"What a coincidence. I teach in Kansas City. Do you have a specialty?"

He nodded. "Divorce law."

"I see," Hannah said, realizing that if she'd married Paul as planned, she'd probably have needed a divorce attorney herself.

Her intention to loosen Jake up a bit wasn't working. He continued to study the road as if he were on an alien planet. "Do you enjoy your work?" she prodded.

"Most of the time. But helping couples dissolve marriages and divide up children and possessions gets pretty brutal. Some people go to great lengths to get revenge." He shot Hannah a sobering glance. "And these are people who once loved each other."

Hannah was almost sorry she'd gotten Jake's attention. His career didn't seem a good diversion. She'd better change the subject. "Is there a Mrs. Reynolds?" she asked. While Jake didn't wear a wedding ring, that didn't prove he was single. Not that it mattered.

He grinned. "Yes, there is. A really terrific Mrs. Reynolds."

Hannah felt surprisingly disappointed. Then Jake turned to her and said, "My mother."

Relief replaced her disappointment, but Hannah immediately chastised herself. Jacob Reynolds's marital status was no concern of hers. She was just making conversation.

"I was married once but it didn't work out," he added. "What about you, Hannah? Are you married?"

She swallowed hard. "No, I'm not."

"Ever come close?"

"Just once."

Hannah choked back the lump that rose in her throat. She couldn't tell Jake that today was supposed to be the first day of her honeymoon. She suddenly felt lonely and sad.

"Well, you're one smart lady. Let me give you some advice that will save you lots of grief. Stay single."

As they drove on in silence, Hannah continued to ponder her current dilemma. She'd come within an hour of marrying a man who would have wanted to rule her life in the same manner her father had ruled her mother's. And she hadn't even realized her mistake until it was almost too late.

Jake seemed in better spirits now but Hannah's had dampened considerably. "Since we aren't serving dinner on the grounds tonight, would you like to stop for a sandwich?" he asked. "Burger Heaven's just ahead. They have the best fast food around."

Hannah brightened a bit. "That sounds good." When she felt really discouraged, nothing lifted her spirits like a burger and fries.

After Jake parked the Bronco, they entered the restaurant and walked up to the counter. "I'll have your double deluxe, jumbo fries, and a chocolate malt," Hannah said. She paid the cashier, then stepped aside so Jake could order.

"Grilled chicken and a side salad with fat-free ranch. And a glass of water, please."

Great. A health food nut. Now she couldn't even indulge in this greasy meal without feeling guilty.

Hannah and Jake settled at a small table by the window to wait for their order. Even the Bronco hadn't confined them the way this tiny table did. Sitting so close to Jake made her very uncomfortable.

She twisted sideways, trying to take up as little room as possible. The appealing scent of Jake's after-shave wasn't helping any. It made Hannah think of cool forests and gentle breezes. When he picked up their order and brought it to the table, Hannah tried to focus her attention on the meal and forget about her handsome dinner partner.

Jake unwrapped his grilled chicken while she slipped the paper off her double deluxe. She nearly gasped when she saw it. The sandwich was the size of a Frisbee! Using both hands, she squished it together so it wouldn't appear quite so large. French fries mounded on her tray like a spilled container of Tinkertoys, and she could barely see Jake over the top of her chocolate malt.

He took a bite of his sandwich. "This really isn't your last meal, Hannah," he said wryly, a crooked grin stealing across his face. "Harold, our camp cook, prepares some pretty tasty dishes. He's a gruff old guy, a retired Army sergeant. But it never takes the kids long to figure out that Harold has a big heart."

"Who else is on staff?" Hannah asked, trying to get excited about her future and push the pain of her past aside.

"You met Desiree, who handles fitness classes and the waterfront. Mrs. Mullins manages the dining hall and KP. She worked as a guard in a women's prison before she retired and started volunteering at camp. Mrs. Mullins knows how to keep kids in line.''

''I'll bet she does,'' Hannah said.

Jake took a sip of water as Hannah enjoyed some of her malt. ''We also have a married couple, Ron and Linda Simpson,'' he continued. ''Linda's the counselor for the girls' cabin, and Ron for the boys' The Simpsons have a dysfunctional marriage, but they're devoted to Camp Wildwood. They come back every summer. And last, there's David Sutton, our nurse.''

Nice group, Hannah thought. A divorce attorney, a retired Army sergeant, a female bodybuilder, a prison guard, a dysfunctional married couple, and a male nurse. Add one runaway bride and you had all the characters for a bizarre situation comedy.

''I can't wait to meet everyone,'' she said, unable to fathom what lay ahead.

She'd been eating fast, trying to finish her meal at the same time as Jake. But she'd only eaten half of her double deluxe when Jake took the last bite of his chicken sandwich. ''Care for some fries?'' she asked, hoping he'd help out.

''No, thanks. I work sixty-hour weeks in my law practice and grab most of my meals on the run. During my days at camp, I try to eat healthy and exercise. Harold humors me by fixing extra vegetables.'' With that comment, he speared the last bit of lettuce with his plastic fork.

Jake's dark eyes had scrutinized her ever since

they'd settled at this tiny table. Now he'd finished eating and she still had half a meal to go. Hannah felt self-conscious under his steady gaze. ''I'll get a to-go box,'' she said, heading for the counter.

Jake watched his new activities director walk up to the counter. He admired the graceful, deliberate way she moved and the way her blond hair shimmered around her shoulders. Sitting across from Hannah had proved an aesthetically pleasing experience. Her ivory skin, rosy cheeks, and light-blond hair made him forget the nightmare of their shopping trip. And he liked the way Hannah's blue eyes sparked with interest as they talked.

But he still really doubted her ability to handle the job. The episode with the grasshopper took less than a minute, but it made him uncomfortable about her future as the activities director. Thank goodness the campers hadn't seen the incident. They'd never let her live it down.

Jake sighed. The kids would find out about Hannah soon enough. They'd discover her insect phobia. They'd learn she lived in a storybook cabin. Hannah would soon be the talk of the Camp Wildwood.

For the five years he'd directed camp, things had run like clockwork. Jake prided himself on putting together a terrific staff, people who really knew their stuff. Would all that change with Hannah on board?

She came toward him carrying a large Styrofoam box and put her leftovers into it.

"We'd better get going," he said.

"I'm ready."

Back at camp, Jake helped Hannah haul her purchases to the cabin. As he watched her unload the lace-edged bedding and fancy curtains, he couldn't help but stare at her. Hannah fascinated him. Her delicate beauty and engaging personality made an alluring combination.

She's your employee, Jake reminded himself. He made it a point never to mix business and pleasure. Besides, after Rachel, he had no interest in women, period.

"Staff meeting starts at nine o'clock at the lodge," he told her. "We'll discuss camp strategy. Can you make it?"

Hannah smiled that dazzling smile. "I'll be there with bells on."

Jake smiled. Even that wouldn't surprise him.

Hannah glanced around the tiny cabin, pleased with the improvement. Her efforts had transformed it from a dirty little dump into a reasonably presentable living space. She'd save the serious scrubbing for another day, but even her minimal efforts had made quite a difference.

The bed looked almost inviting—if you could call two wooden bunks full of carved initials and petrified chewing gum inviting. But the comforter and pillow shams had dressed it up nicely.

Hannah hung up her clothes, then slipped the hangers over rusty nails protruding from the cabin's exposed studs, creating an open-air closet of sorts. Her travel clock ticked comfortingly on the small table.

It was 8:30 already. Staff meeting started at nine. She slipped out of her silk blouse and pulled on a T-shirt she'd planned to use as a swimsuit cover-up on her honeymoon. It had a beach scene with palm trees on the front, and under the picture, raised letters that spelled out ISLAND PARADISE.

She sighed. Where would she be right now if she had married Paul? Would they be strolling Waikiki Beach? Swimming in the Pacific? Possibly watching a sunset over Diamond Head?

As she glanced around the dumpy, makeshift cabin, she felt a sinking sensation in the pit of her stomach. Had she acted in haste? Would things have worked out with Paul if she'd tried harder?

Get real, her conscience chided. If she had married Paul, he would be telling her where to stroll, how to swim, and what to look for in the sunset. No, she hadn't made a mistake. She was just nervous about her new job.

Hannah hurried up the hill and entered the lodge where several adults were seated at one of the long tables. She went to join them. Jake stood with one sneakered foot on a bench, clipboard in hand. He wore jeans and a turquoise knit shirt that made his shoulders appear unbelievably broad. He leaned forward, ready to propel into action.

She tried to keep her mind off Jacob's good looks but it wasn't easy. It didn't help matters any when he flashed her that slightly crooked grin. Her palms got sweaty and her heart rate increased.

Hannah chided herself for her adolescent reaction to the camp director's smile, reminding herself— sternly—that this man was her employer. She'd have her hands full trying to function as the activities director without complicating matters with a schoolgirl crush.

Jake smiled at the group. "Welcome, staff members. We're planning another great summer here at Camp Wildwood. As some of you know, Marlene broke her leg and can't join us this summer. I want you to meet our new Activities Director, Hannah Hastings. Hannah, would you stand?"

Hannah stood while the rest of the staff applauded. They looked perfectly normal and seemed friendly enough.

"Hannah signed on today," Jake continued, "and she's trying to get organized. I hope you veterans will show her the ropes."

Then Jake launched into a speech about camp organization and regulations and Hannah felt thankful to be out of the limelight. He hit so heavily on dining hall procedures, bathroom cleanup, and KP that Hannah felt like she'd just enlisted in the Army. Jacob

Reynolds ran a tight ship, that was clear. She hoped she'd be able to meet his expectations.

As Jake continued to expound, Hannah grew sleepy. Her runaway flight from Kansas City and all the accompanying stress was catching up with her. She blinked rapidly, trying with all her might to focus on Jake, who now had four dazzling brown eyes instead of just two. And an extra nose, as well! She batted her eyes feverishly, trying to make his features return to normal.

She had to stay awake till this meeting ended. After all, this was her first official duty as Activities Director. Maybe if she concentrated on something else.

She tried to pick out the various staff members Jake had mentioned at dinner. *Let's see, the stocky, square-shouldered woman must be Mrs. Mullins, who had, no doubt, instilled fear into the prisoners.* Mrs. Mullins sat beside a short, wiry man with a grizzled gray beard who must be the former Army sergeant and camp cook. Jake happened to be bragging about Harold's cooking skills at this very moment. Mrs. Mullins flashed Harold a dazzling smile. Did those two have a little romance going?

Ron and Linda Simpson, the dysfunctional married couple, sat on the same bench, several feet apart. You could have squeezed three campers between them. That left David Sutton, the nurse, who listened intently to Jake's monologue.

The diversion was working. At least she hadn't dozed off and fallen off the bench.

"Hannah?"

Jake's deep voice came at her out of the fog and her heart started pounding. "Yes?"

"Did you hear the question?"

"I'm sorry, I didn't."

He leveled his dark eyes on her. Thankfully now there were only two. "Can you have an activity ready for tomorrow afternoon?"

"Um, sure. I'll have something prepared," she said, not having a clue as to what or how.

"Great. I'll pass out schedules for the week and we'll make adjustments as we go along. Staff breakfast is tomorrow at seven and campers start arriving at ten. Any questions?" Jake gazed around the group expectantly. "If not, that concludes this meeting. Get some rest. The fun starts tomorrow."

The staff crowded around Hannah to introduce themselves and welcome her to Camp Wildwood. After a few minutes of pleasantries, everyone said good night. Hannah pulled a stack of dusty volumes from the bookshelf to help prepare for tomorrow's activity. "Can I help you with those?" Jake offered, coming toward her.

His offer was tempting. Hannah felt a little hesitant about traipsing through the woods in the dark. "Thanks. That would be great," she said as she loaded his arms with several dusty volumes and carried several herself.

As they left the lodge, Hannah stumbled along beside her new employer. Obviously, sandals weren't appropriate footwear for the Arkansas Ozarks, but that was all she had.

"It's certainly dark tonight," she said. "I wish I'd remembered my flashlight."

"They come in handy," Jake said, striding along beside her.

A variety of insects began nibbling at Hannah's ankles and she swatted them away.

"More grasshoppers?" he teased.

"I'm quite certain these are mosquitoes."

"Did you put on insect repellent?"

"I forgot."

"You'll remember it tomorrow."

When they reached her cabin and Hannah flipped on the light, the pine aerosol and the mold were having it out with each other and she couldn't tell who was winning. "Just set those on the table."

After they'd put down their books, Hannah walked Jake to the door. He lingered a moment and she thought about offering him a Coke but that might not be proper etiquette. "Thanks for your help today. Especially for giving me the job."

He nodded. "You're welcome."

"I'll try to meet your expectations."

"I'm sure you will. See you in the morning." Jake

Reynolds opened the screen door and disappeared into the darkness.

Hannah sighed. She looked around the small cabin that looked a little more appealing in the dim light and flipped open the first book, which added to the mold already permeating the room. She turned its brittle pages, staring at an assortment of wildflowers. But she felt too tired to concentrate.

How could her life have changed so radically in just twenty-four hours? She'd gone from an almost-married woman to a permanently single one, she'd landed a job she wasn't qualified for, and she'd moved into a cabin that would comfortably house only one of the seven dwarves.

Her life was out of balance. Like a pinball machine on tilt. While she knew she'd made the right choice by not marrying Paul, there was still a deep sense of loss. Loss of a carefully planned future, if nothing else. She sighed again. Had she made things better or worse by signing on as Camp Wildwood's activities director?

One thing she did know. She'd better watch out for her new employer. Hannah wanted to forget that great-looking men shared the planet with her. That was a pretty tough assignment with Jacob Reynolds around.

She gazed at the book, pushing all thoughts of Jake aside. As she paged through drawings of trees, wild-flowers, birds, and rocks, she wondered how on earth she'd learn all these different species by tomorrow morning.

Suddenly she spotted the Styrofoam box from Burger Heaven resting on the top bunk where she'd left it. Comfort food! Hannah climbed the shaky ladder, settled herself on the top bunk, and nibbled at the remains of her double deluxe and fries. They were cold and she'd kill for a microwave, but her new home wasn't equipped with such luxuries.

The food revived her. Maybe she'd shower tonight, then set her alarm early and prepare for the nature hike first thing tomorrow morning. She grabbed the gown she'd purchased for her wedding night, gathered up towels, soap, and shampoo, and headed for the bathhouse. This time she remembered her flashlight.

As Jake started to leave the men's bathhouse after his shower, he saw Hannah coming out of the women's. When she stepped into the area illumined by the floodlight, Jake caught his breath.

Hannah's sun-blond hair gleamed in the eerie, incandescent light. She wore a pretty gown and dainty, backless slippers that looked like they belonged in a Saks Fifth Avenue display window. Hannah looked surreally beautiful—like a wood nymph that had just slipped out of the forest.

She noticed him and stopped. "Oh, um, hello again."

"Hi. How was your shower?" Stupid question, but his brain wasn't functioning just right.

"Great. The shower was great," she said, trying to

juggle her clothing, a wet towel, and her assortment of toiletries.

"Do you need help getting this stuff back to your cabin?"

"No, thanks. I can manage. Good night."

"Good night," he said.

Jake watched Hannah walk toward her cabin. When he could no longer see her, he watched the beam of her flashlight bounce along the wooded path. After both Hannah and her ray of light disappeared, Jake expelled his breath, unaware until this moment he'd been holding it.

He turned and walked toward his cabin, lost in thought. He couldn't believe his runaway attraction to his new employee. Since his divorce from Rachel, he'd hardly dated. Hadn't had any desire to. His job, and trying to be both father and mother to Aaron, took all his time and energy.

Several of his buddies at the law firm occasionally fixed him up. And while the women were attractive, witty, and bright, they hadn't stirred any longings inside him.

Not so with Hannah. She sparked something inside Jake he wanted to keep buried.

His job as camp director was all-consuming. Helping thirty-five inner-city kids have a good camping experience called for his undivided attention. He couldn't afford to get sidetracked—by anything or anybody.

As he entered his small cabin and hung his bath towel on a nail, the image of Hannah standing in the eerie circle of light outside the bathhouse flashed into his consciousness. The moment had seemed unreal. Almost dreamlike. He wondered if it really happened or if he just imagined it.

He brushed the memory aside and pushed Hannah Hastings out of his thoughts. A busload of kids would arrive tomorrow morning at 10:00 and he'd better be ready.

Chapter Three

Kids started streaming into the lodge. They came individually and in small groups and the screen door banged shut so many times that it sounded to Hannah like the methodical popping of a bunch of balloons.

A few of the kids wore designer shirts and shorts but most were dressed in faded T-shirts and grubby cutoffs. They looked tough. Like street kids. One had a tattoo on his arm that said NO FEAR. Many wore earrings—and over half of them were boys!

Maybe Jake was right. Maybe she couldn't handle these kids. They were light years away from her kindergartners.

And she felt quite uncomfortable in the woods. The mosquitoes found her a particularly succulent snack, and the squirrels startled her as they skittered out of nowhere when she walked a path alone.

If that wasn't enough to depress her, Hannah also felt lonely. All her plans and dreams had evaporated. No wedding. No Hawaiian honeymoon. If Paul hadn't been such a control freak, she'd be in Honolulu right now, instead of in the Ozarks with these hoodlum kids.

And the biggest problem of all was her totally irrational attraction to Jake. Maybe she wouldn't experience it today. Maybe she was better rested and more in control of her tattered nerves.

At that moment, Jake came out of his office, walked to the front of the lodge, and blew his whistle into the noisy confusion. Tanned, muscular, and gorgeous pretty well summed up her new employer.

"Welcome to Camp Wildwood, boys and girls." Jake's deep voice cut through the chaos and the kids quieted. "I'm Mr. Reynolds, your Camp Director. Since we'll be spending lots of time together this summer, we need to get better acquainted. So first, I'll introduce our staff."

Jake proceeded to present Harold, Mrs. Mullins, Dave, Desiree, and the Simpsons, who were holding hands today. *Must be one of their better days,* Hannah thought. "And last, but not least," Jake continued, "our Activities Director, Miss Hastings."

Several older boys let loose with shrill wolf whistles. And one yelled, "Whoa! What a babe!"

Nope. This was nothing like teaching kindergarten.

Jake's intense brown eyes fastened expectantly on Hannah and she had the identical feelings that he'd stirred up yesterday. Maybe she'd better see a shrink. Her body had obviously taken her brain hostage.

"Would you tell the campers what you're planning, Miss Hastings?" Jake asked.

Hannah stood. "I'd be glad to. We're going to have lots of fun this summer, kids. Our first activity will be a nature hike. And after the hike, we'll come back to the lodge and iron the leaves that you collect between sheets of waxed paper. We'll also going to have lots of campfires this summer and learn to square-dance."

"Square-dance?" one boy called out. "Are you nuts?"

Jake was on the kid in the blink of an eye. "That's disrespectful, Aaron. Stand up and apologize to Miss Hastings."

The boy didn't move a muscle.

Jake's eyes drilled into the child. "This minute."

Aaron stood and stared down at his sneakers. "Sorry, Miss Hastings," he mumbled.

Hannah's heartbeat accelerated. She'd expected confrontation but not quite so soon.

Jake coughed nervously as Hannah continued discussing her plans. This was going to be even worse than he'd imagined. Hannah planned to have this bunch of ruffians square-dancing and ironing leaves. That was like inviting Jesse James's gang to tea.

After finishing the orientation session, Jake dismissed the campers and they scurried to the lunch line. He walked toward Hannah who looked particularly attractive in a red-and-white-and-blue shorts set. Her tanned legs tapered gracefully into a pair of red-white-and-blue sandals that showed off nice straight toes with a perfect pedicure and bright red polish. Bright, bright red polish. Hannah could be Miss Fourth of July at a company picnic.

"Are you hungry?" Jake asked, pretty sure he already knew the answer.

"Starving. By the time I got my lesson plans finished, Harold had closed the breakfast line."

"Come on, then. We're having taco salad."

They moved along in the chow line and finally reached the serving area. Harold flashed Jake a smile. "Howdy, Captain. All set for another great summer?"

"You bet."

Jake did feel excited about the days he spent at Camp Wildwood. As a divorce lawyer, he saw what happened to children when their families split up, and it wasn't always pleasant. A number of his campers came from single-parent homes, and managing this camp was an opportunity to give something back.

Everything was moving on course. His only concern was whether his new activities director could handle the job.

Jake led Hannah to the far end of the dining hall, away from the worst of the racket, and sat down across from her. "Your plans sound interesting. But I was wondering if you've ever led a nature hike?"

As she studied him over a forkful of taco salad, her azure eyes made his heart skip a beat. They were as clear as a mountain stream and had great potential to distract him. "Not exactly," she replied.

Just as he suspected. If Hannah's first activity flopped, her credibility would be impaired. Kids could be very unforgiving. "Would it help if we did a test run?"

She laid her fork down but didn't take her eyes off him. "A test run?"

"Yeah. I thought we could take a hike after lunch. I can help you identify any wildflowers and trees you're unfamiliar with. Sort of a rehearsal for the actual event."

She cleared her throat. "You mean just the two of us?"

He cleared his, too. "Yes."

"Alone?"

"Is that a problem?"

Hannah's eyes were as big as silver dollars and the most beautiful thing Jake had ever encountered.

"No. No problem. It's a great idea."

When they'd finished eating, Jake asked, "Are you ready?"

She nodded. But as he glanced at her tray he knew something was wrong. Hannah had barely touched her taco salad.

* * *

As Hannah headed into the woods, Jake just two steps behind her, she determined to be fully objective. This expedition into the wilderness with her handsome employer was nothing more than a tutoring session. Because Jake wanted her to succeed in her job, he was coaching her. Well, she certainly needed all the help she could get.

As they ventured deeper into the woods, the only sounds marring the stillness were crackling twigs that snapped beneath their feet. The air felt damp and cool and smelled of wet leaves. Hannah inhaled deeply, realizing she'd better figure out a way to commune with nature, and fast. Her job depended on it.

"Watch out for that branch." Jake pulled back a huge limb that partially blocked the path. As Hannah slipped past him, she held her breath, knowing if she didn't, Jake's scent would envelop her, drowning out everything else.

As they made their way through the trees, bright sun rays filtered down. A bird called "jay, jay" from a branch overhead and Jake gazed skyward. "Can you identify that bird?"

"Of course. It's a blue jay. Every student in my class knows a blue jay when they see one."

He grinned crookedly. "I actually meant the other bird."

Hannah peered up into the trees, shading her eyes from the flashes of sunlight that streamed down. But there wasn't another feathered friend in sight. "I don't see another bird."

He put his finger to his lips. "Just listen to its call."

She listened and heard a low-pitched *yank, yank, yank, yank.* "Don't tell me that's a bird? It sounds like it has postnasal drip."

He chuckled. "It's a white-breasted nuthatch, Hannah. This specie of nuthatch looks a lot like a black-capped chickadee. But the black-capped chickadee has a whistled call with the second tone a full note lower than the first."

Uh-oh. Looked like they'd surpassed the kindergarten level of bird identification and moved right on up to graduate school.

They started walking and Hannah continued to gaze upward, hoping to get a glimpse of the white-breasted nuthatch.

"Watch out," Jake cautioned. "There's a stream just ahead."

A stream of crystal-clear water appeared out of nowhere. "How lovely," Hannah said.

"Let me go first. Then I'll help you across."

The stream looked awfully wide but Jake crossed it easily. "Here," he said. "Take my hand."

She stretched her arm out as far as she could and Jake's strong fingers gripped hers. "Jump!"

Hannah mustered every ounce of strength she could and jumped. Jake pulled and with both their efforts, she almost cleared the stream. Unfortunately, her sandals came smacking down at the edge of it, splattering her legs with icy cold water. And horror of horrors, Jake's legs got splattered, too.

"I'm so sorry." She pulled a tissue from her pocket and handed it to him.

Jake shook his head. "It's okay, Hannah. I've been wet before."

She tried to smile but her face suddenly felt frozen. This nature hike wasn't going well. Hannah sighed. "Looks like I have a lot to learn before tomorrow morning."

"It takes time," Jake said. "But with what you learn today and the studying you do tonight, you'll do fine. Look, Hannah," he said, pointing to the ground up ahead.

Jake crouched down and Hannah was surprised to see him cradle a delicate blossom between his fingers. "It's beautiful," she said, kneeling beside him to admire the colorful flowers. "They're violets."

"*Viola pedata* is their scientific name. Their common name is birdsfoot violets."

She shook her head in frustration.

"Don't you like them?" Jake asked.

"I love them. But it would help if they didn't add the word *bird* to the names of flowers. I'm having enough trouble keeping all these species straight."

Jake smiled and Hannah's heart warmed at his smile.

As Jake admired the blossom with its light blue

lower petals and deep purple upper ones, they reminded him of Hannah's lovely eyes. He'd noticed the
same delicate shading there. He stood abruptly and
squared his shoulders. When he started gazing at flowers and seeing Hannah's eyes, things were spiraling
out of control "We'd better get back to camp," he
said brusquely.

Jake felt suddenly claustrophobic—as if the woods
were closing in on him. He'd always enjoyed hiking.
He found strength in the towering trees and enjoyed
identifying birdcalls. And he marveled at the dainty
wildflowers dotting color along the path.

But he found no peace here today. Being with Hannah stirred up emotions he didn't want to confront.
"I'm sorry to cut our hike short," he said, "but Desiree could use some help at the waterfront."

"That's all right. I'm ready to head back anyway."

"Come on, then. I know a shortcut."

On the walk back, Jake pointed out various plants
and trees, rattling off their species, trying to lose himself in the wonder of the woods. But it just wasn't
working.

When he spotted the parting of the trees that sig-
naled their return to camp, he breathed a relieved sigh.
"Do you have any questions?"

"Not particularly. I hope I can make the nature hike
interesting for the kids."

Jake almost reached over to smooth the furrows
from Hannah's forehead that normally looked so satin

smooth. He stopped himself just in time. "Don't worry. Most of the campers can't tell sweet William from Bermuda grass."

Her slight smile tugged at his heart. Hurriedly, Jake turned and they walked the remaining distance. When they parted company, he headed for his office. Maybe in that small, musty cubicle, he'd be able to concentrate on his work. He certainly couldn't manage it in the forest. Not with Hannah by his side.

Being alone with Hannah had reminded him of his early days with Rachel. Rachel's fresh beauty and appealing ways had stolen Jake's heart. A short time later, they'd married, and as far as Jake was concerned, it was forever.

But Rachel's commitment wasn't as serious. One summer afternoon, he'd come home early from work to find her packing. He couldn't believe it when she told him she couldn't stand the confines of marriage anymore and was leaving him and Aaron.

Well, he knew better now. He wouldn't fall in love again. After some agonizing times, he'd gotten his and Aaron's lives back on track. No woman would ever hurt them again.

Pushing all thoughts of Hannah aside, Jake grabbed the stack of mail on his desk. As he sorted through it, he reminded himself that he was a single father and he intended to stay that way.

*   *   *

The minute Hannah entered the noisy lodge, she could tell that Jake was in his usual top-notch form. He wore a yellow knit shirt that showed off his terrific tan, and a pair of stonewashed blue jeans. She thanked her lucky stars that for once his great-looking legs were tucked under a layer of denim.

Jake blew his whistle and the noisy kids settled down. "Quiet, campers. Miss Hastings is ready to give instructions for your nature hike."

As she came to the front of the room, Jake took the whistle from around his neck and slipped in into Hannah's hand. Her heart skipped a beat at the contact. "Maybe this will help," he said.

"Thanks," she replied, trying to ignore the fact that his warm touch made her senses spring to attention. *Stay focused,* she reminded herself. Taking a ragged breath, she turned to face the little ruffians.

"Everyone find a partner. You'll stay with your partner throughout the hike."

It took considerable effort, but finally all the campers were paired up. Jake came to whisper in her ear. "Would it help if I came along?"

"Came along?" Hannah repeated the words like a mindless parrot. Jake's staying behind was the only good thing about the whole event. But she couldn't very well tell him not to come. "If you like," she said, struggling to make her voice sound normal. Forcing her attention back to the kids, she said, "All right, campers. Let's go."

Hannah and Jake led the noisy pack out of the lodge, across the open field, and into the woods. As they forged ahead, the path narrowed. A furry animal darted out of the underbrush and skittered across Hannah's sandal. She tried to swallow the scream that welled up in her throat. Fortunately, she managed. "What on earth was that?" she cried.

"A rat, Miss Hastings," one of kids called. "We have lots of rats where I live."

"That was no rat," Jake said impatiently. "It was a chipmunk. A harmless little chipmunk."

"Oh, thank goodness." Hannah's pulse beat like a bass drum. She imagined she could still feel the animal's warm body and its tiny toenails. But she smiled up at Jake, as if having a rodent run across your feet was a perfectly normal occurrence.

"Look, kids," she said, spotting a plant with a cluster of white flowers at the top of the stem. "That's sweet Wilbur."

"Sweet William," Jake corrected.

Hannah flushed. "That's what I meant to say. Sweet William."

They walked a ways farther and she tried again. "This tree is a white walnut."

Jake nodded.

Bolstered by her success she added, "Some trees like elm trees have a single leaf. But others, like this white walnut, have several parts to each leaf. They're called complex leaves."

Jake was shaking his head. "Compound leaves," he whispered.

"Correction. The white walnut tree has *compound* leaves."

By now, the names of the various species she'd memorized were swimming together in her head. Was the yellow-bellied flycatcher a small bird or an insect-eating plant? Did the tufted titmouse have feathers or a long tail?

When the path widened, Jake came to walk beside her, making concentration even more difficult.

In addition to trying to ignore Jake's powerful presence, Hannah tried to disregard the uprising going on behind her. "You let go of that branch on purpose," screamed one of the campers.

"I did not!"

"I'll never be your partner again, jerk-face!"

The trees parted to reveal a valley and a trickling stream. "Why don't you turn the kids loose and let them collect their leaves?" Jake suggested.

Hannah made the announcement and the campers spread across the valley like honey on warm bread. The sun shone down warmly. Jake's muscular arms, incredibly tanned and covered with shiny black hair, made quite a contrast to her own fair skin. She'd started freckling furiously the moment she arrived at camp. Maybe if she pieced enough freckles together, they'd turn into a gorgeous tan, like his. "I'm not sure how much the kids are learning," she said.

"Now that they're collecting their own leaves, they'll learn even more," Jake responded. "You can help them identify their leaves."

And reindeer can fly, Hannah thought dismally. "I brought one of the reference books along so the kids can look up their own species. They'll remember more if they do the work themselves."

Jake brightened. "Good idea."

His approval washed over her like soothing balm. After the campers collected their leaves, they clustered around Hannah and Jake, passing the reference book around eagerly. Hannah breathed a relieved sigh. Something was finally going right.

"This leaf came from a hickory tree," Herbert explained. "And that one's a red maple."

"Very good," Hannah coached.

"What kind of plant is this?" Aaron asked. He held a bouquet that contained greenish flowers, white berries, and leaves arranged in clusters of three.

Susan thumbed through the book trying to identify the species. "This one is—" She shrieked. "It's poison ivy! Aaron! You picked poison ivy!"

"How was I supposed to know it was poison ivy?" He turned to Lindy. "Here, Lindy, I picked this just for you." He stuck the bouquet in the girl's face and she ran off, screaming.

Hannah jumped to her feet and grabbed Aaron's arm. "Teasing Lindy that way was uncalled for. Now put that poison ivy down and go wash your hands in the stream. You're in big trouble, young man.''

As the boy followed her instructions, Hannah realized that her taste of success was short-lived. ''Maybe we'd better head back to the lodge,'' she told Jake.

''That's probably a good idea.''

''Everyone find your partner.''

For the moment, Hannah wasn't sure which way to turn. ''Do we go to the left?'' she whispered to Jake.

''Not if you want to get back to Pine Bluff Lodge. I'll lead them back, Hannah.''

She sighed, thankful that the horrible hike was nearly over. ''Follow Mr. Reynolds, campers.''

Under Jake's leadership, the return trip went smoothly. Hannah caught occasional glimpses of him up ahead, leading the campers with unfaltering steps.

Back at the lodge, they ironed their leaves and ran into a few complications. When Lindy picked up the hot iron, it slipped from her grasp. She caught it by the cord and it dangled precariously until Hannah helped her get it back onto the table. Then Herbert accidentally ironed his index finger. The noise level swelled out of control.

Once again, chaos reigned. Hannah solved the problem by dismissing the campers to swimming class.

Everyone left the lodge except Jake, the last person on earth she wanted to be alone with. She sighed. ''We ran into a few snags.''

He didn't disagree. "Listen, I've got to run into town to pick up supplies. See you later."

While Jake hadn't openly criticized her, Hannah figured he wasn't exactly pleased.

She sighed. Why would he be? She hadn't recognized a poison ivy bouquet!

Chapter Four

Hannah couldn't quite face the confines of her musty little cottage. Maybe a stroll around the lake would lift her spirits. As she set out on her journey, she followed a well-worn path that edged the periphery of Lake Wildwood. The evening air was hot but a breeze made it bearable.

The bright orange sun slipped lower in the sky, duplicating its neon image in the rippling water. Frogs croaked loudly and Hannah half expected a troop of them to lunge at her out of the great unknown. As she walked along, the stress of the day began to dissipate. She breathed deeply, filling her lungs with the fresh, clean air. Just as she was beginning to feel at peace with herself and almost at one with nature, she noticed someone in the distance. As the figure approached, she recognized the surefooted gait and the well-muscled body that belonged to Jacob Reynolds.

He spotted her and waved, and as she waved back, all her newfound peace slipped away like a discarded snakeskin.

He came to stand beside her. ''Are you going to the Point?''

''Where is the Point?''

''Just a little walk from here. It's a beautiful spot, especially at sunset.''

Hannah forced a smile. ''Then I'd better check it out.''

''Maybe I'll come along. You might get lost.''

Hannah considered arguing the point but decided against it. She'd been lost once today already.

They moved on in silence. Finally, Jake asked, ''How did you end up at Camp Wildwood, Hannah?''

She took a steadying breath, trying to decide how much to tell him. ''Teachers always need summer jobs,'' she said. ''I had plans for the summer but they fell through. One thing led to another and I ended up here.''

''So you had another job lined up?''

''Sort of,'' she replied, not wanting to tell him the whole, sordid story.

As they continued walking, Hannah suddenly needed a confidant. And Jake was the only person she knew in the entire state of Arkansas. ''I'd planned to be married this summer," she confessed. "But at the last minute, things didn't work out."

Jake stopped and turned to face her and Hannah saw compassion flash into his dark, intriguing eyes. "I'm sorry, Hannah. That must have been a shock."

"Yes, it was."

They resumed their slow walking. "Well, better now than later. I don't want to sound unfeeling, but most marriages don't last. It used to be twenty-five percent that failed, then forty percent. Now over half of all marriages end in divorce. The odds were not in your favor."

She sighed. "I know the statistics are discouraging but I still believe that if the right people find each other, their marriage has a chance. Not only to survive, but to be happy."

"I'm not so sure," Jake countered. "If you spent one day in my office, you'd agree. One of my clients, a prosperous business man, had only been married six months when his young wife filed for divorce and got a huge settlement. My client will pay for that mistake for the rest of his life."

So much for comfort, Hannah thought, not particularly interested in the misery of Jake's clients. She had quite enough misery of her own.

"We've almost reached the Point," Jake said. "There's a bench where we can watch the sunset. If you have time."

Talking with Jake—being with Jake—confused her more than ever.

They reached the bench and sat in silence as the flaming sun sank in the darkening sky. A pair of ducks skimmed the lake's surface, the male's colors brilliant, the female's more subdued. The two moved upward, circling gracefully. They flew just inches apart, their bodies gliding in perfect formation. "How magnificent," Hannah observed. "What kind of ducks are they?"

"Mallards."

"What unity." She shook her head. "Why can't people do that?"

"I wish I knew. Animals have an innate sense about relating that people don't seem to have. Too bad, isn't it?"

Jake turned to face her and the look in his eyes made Hannah's breathing turn shallow. His face was just inches from hers, well within kissing range.

When Jake slipped his arm around her shoulders, Hannah tried to say they'd better head back to camp. But she couldn't force a word past the lump in her throat. As he touched her shoulder, the warmth of his hand, and the thrill of pleasure his touch ignited, made Hannah's heart race.

Jake placed both hands gently on her shoulders, holding her captive. Not with his hands, but with his magnificent eyes.

"Maybe we should . . ."

Before she could finish the sentence, Jake bent toward her and kissed her. Hannah's heart beat so fast, it was as if sparklers, Roman candles, and cherry bombs seemed to erupt in her chest.

Knowing better, she moved into Jake's embrace and laced her arms around his neck. She shouldn't return Jake's kiss. It would just make matters worse. But she couldn't make herself pull away. The kiss built with each passing moment, and just when it reached a dimension of wonder Hannah had never before experienced, she heard it.

Snickering. It was definitely snickering. She'd taught kindergarten long enough to recognize snickering when she heard it. Jake pulled away. Obviously, he'd heard it, too.

"Go for it, Mr. Reynolds," a child's voice encouraged. "Like you said this morning, we need to get better acquainted."

Jake sprang to his feet and took out after the youngsters, who scampered into the woods like startled rabbits. Moments later, he strode back and towered over Hannah. He ran his fingers through his hair and paced in front of the bench where they had just shared a kiss. Not even a smidgen of tenderness was left in his dark brown eyes. Just fury and frustration.

"Darn kids," he said gruffly. "They know they're not to come this far from camp unescorted. Especially at night."

Hannah tried to stop her head from spinning, tried

to get her pulse rate back within normal range. She started to stand, but her legs buckled so she sank back onto the bench.

"We'd better go." Jake's matter-of-fact tone erased all remnants of the romantic mood that had caused Hannah to lose track of all reason.

The fiery sun suddenly slipped below the horizon and a cool breeze stirred the trees. As the two of them walked back to the campgrounds, an awkward, uncomfortable silence reigned. The magic had disappeared as abruptly as if a candle had been blown out.

Hannah took a deep breath and let it out slowly. "Maybe whoever spied on us will keep this to themselves."

Jake's chuckle was sardonic. "Dream on, Hannah. We'll have to live this down. And I promise you it won't be easy." He walked her home and mumbled a casual "Good night."

After he'd gone, Hannah sat on the front step of her cabin reconstructing the moments she and Jake had shared at the Point.

How could she have let him kiss her? The picturesque setting and the attraction she felt for her new employer caused her to lose perspective. She'd just started getting her life back on track, and the feeling of independence was freeing. Yet within days, she'd kissed Jake, on a park bench, no less. To make matters worse, they'd been observed. Rumors about Mr. Reynolds and Miss Hastings would spread like wildfire through Camp Wildwood, making life here even more difficult.

Hannah sighed. What troubled her most about this new development was the powerful emotion she felt while Jake held her in his arms.

Hannah waited nervously in the breakfast line, hoping she wouldn't run into Jake. Last night, she'd lain awake until late reliving the magic moments when Jake had kissed her. When she finally drifted off to sleep, Jake's kiss maintained center stage, swirling its way through her dreams.

She carried her breakfast tray over to a table full of kids, wondering what their response would be.

"Morning, Miss Hastings," came the ragged chorus. They went on with their chatter and didn't pay her any special attention.

Several minutes later, Lindy turned to her. "I guess you heard about Aaron."

What had Aaron done now? Burned down the boys' cabin? "No," she replied. "What happened to Aaron?"

"He's in the infirmary. He has poison ivy all over his body." Lindy smirked. "Serves him right."

"Who told you?"

"His father."

"You mean Aaron's father drove all the way to camp? Just because he has poison ivy?"

Lindy sighed impatiently. "No, Miss Hastings. Aaron's father is already here. It's Mr. Reynolds."

Hannah choked on her orange juice. "You mean Jake . . . Mr. Reynolds . . . is Aaron's father?"

"Of course. Everyone knows that," Herbert said smugly.

Everyone but her.

Hannah suddenly saw yesterday's difficulties in a new light. Aaron, her biggest problem kid, was the camp director's son. And she had threatened to punish the boy for the poison ivy incident. Was Jake upset with her for disciplining his son?

After breakfast, Hannah headed for the infirmary and her knock was answered by the camp director himself. A white T-shirt with rolled-up sleeves and jean shorts showed off his muscular body. He looked terrific, except for his expression, which was guarded.

She cleared her throat. "I hear Aaron has poison ivy."

Jake pushed open the screen door. "Yeah. He's one uncomfortable kid. See for yourself."

Aaron, propped up by several bed pillows, lay stretched out on a cot. Angry blisters coated his arms and legs and his face contained a number of red welts. David Sutton sat beside him, dabbing on calamine lotion. The lotion turned Aaron's skin as pink as a newborn's.

"That does it, young man," David said when he

finished the task. "If I were you, I'd stay away from poison ivy. Think you'll recognize it next time?"

Aaron nodded. "I'll never forget what poison ivy looks like." He squirmed. "Or feels like, either."

David turned to Jake. "I'd like Aaron to stay here until lunchtime so I can keep an eye on him. He has a pretty severe case."

"Fine. Thanks for your help, David," Jake said.

As Hannah and Jake stepped out into the bright June sunshine, he said, "I need to talk to you. If you have a minute."

"Sure," she said, waiting for the next bomb to drop.

"Let's go sit on the retaining wall."

Hannah followed Jake over to an old stone wall. He boosted himself up easily and while Hannah made several attempts, she couldn't quite manage. "Need some help?" he asked.

"No, thanks."

She didn't want Jake's help. Didn't want him to put his strong hands around her waist. Didn't want to be inundated by his aftershave, or get any closer to those tantalizing eyes. But she just couldn't manage by herself. "I guess I need a boost."

Jake sprang down and circled her waist with his hands and with one fluid motion lifted her onto the wall. He joined her and when he sighed audibly, Hannah figured she was in trouble. His words caught her off guard. "I've been unfair to you, Hannah."

She shifted her position. "Unfair? What do you mean?"

"I've expected you to do a job you aren't trained for."

"I suppose you could say that."

"However," he continued, "I'm sure we can make this work if we try a little harder."

"Oh?"

"You just need more supervision."

Hannah's heart sank. Jake sounded just like Paul. Paul had always wanted to supervise, dominate, and manipulate. "I know I had some problems yesterday, but it was my first activity."

"I realize that. But if you and I meet regularly and do some troubleshooting, we can head off problems before they arise. Now, what's your next activity?"

Hannah sighed, feeling defensive and disappointed. But if she wanted to keep her job, she'd have to play the game by Jake's rules. "I'm planning a campfire for tomorrow night. First, I'll teach the kids some camp songs, then we'll have a few skits." She stared at him coolly. "I don't anticipate any problems, Jake." What did he think she'd do? Set the woods on fire?

He nodded. "That's a good start."

As Hannah talked about her campfire plans, Jake listened patiently, wondering if she could possibly pull it off. "And finally," she continued, "I'll close with a few inspirational thoughts."

"A sermon?" he asked. "You plan to preach the kids a sermon?"

"Of course not. I just want to leave them with some uplifting ideas."

This little talk wasn't working. While Hannah had accepted his offer of help without much resistance, there were other problems. For one thing, Jake had great difficulty concentrating with Hannah sitting so close. Her gardenia perfume flooded his senses, taking him back to the moments they shared at the Point. He remembered how incredibly good it felt to take Hannah into his arms and kiss her.

As Hannah studied him, her azure eyes drilled into his very soul. "You don't need to worry, Jake. I can conduct a darned good campfire. It's very different from a nature hike. I don't anticipate any problems," she continued, unaware of the battle raging inside him.

"All right. We'll go with the campfire." He cleared his throat. "And you don't object to discussing your plans with me ahead of time?"

"I suppose not." Her lips pouted slightly and Jake again thought about kissing her.

She sighed. "I wish you'd trust my judgment."

"I do trust your judgment," Jake said, wondering if you could be struck by lightning on a sunny day if you stretched the truth far enough. "I just want more input, that's all."

"Okay then. We'll discuss my plans ahead of

time,'' Hannah said softly. ''No more surprises. Does that satisfy you?''

He nodded. ''That satisfies me.''

But it wasn't true. The only thing that would satisfy him right now would be to take Hannah in his arms and kiss her as thoroughly as he'd kissed her at the Point last night. That kiss stirred feelings inside him no woman had ever brought out. Not even Rachel.

He'd better watch himself. What he felt for Hannah was powerful. *You can't afford to fall in love again,* he reminded himself. He and Aaron were just beginning to rebuild a stable life after the turmoil of Rachel's leaving. He wouldn't risk that stability. Not for anyone.

Not even for Hannah.

The kids gathered at the campfire site, hauling their blankets with them. They giggled and shouted and pushed in their usual fashion but finally managed to spread their blankets around the neat tower of logs Jake had constructed earlier that afternoon.

Hannah had worked hard planning tonight's campfire. If it went smoothly, Jake might overlook some of her earlier mistakes.

He appeared and spread his blanket off to one side. As usual, his presence stirred up a host of emotions in her: fear, excitement, longing, delight, inadequacy, panic, and a bit of yearning. Jacob Reynolds was the seven deadly sins personified.

He caught Hannah's eye and smiled, increasing her heart rate and turning her palms slightly damp. His ability to set her heart pounding with a just smile or glance unnerved her. She smiled back, praying all would go smoothly tonight.

When Mrs. Mullins arrived, Hannah knew everything would be fine. She'd talked to the woman earlier in the day and asked her to help maintain order during campfire. Mrs. Mullins spread her blanket behind some of the rowdiest kids and gave Hannah a conspiratorial nod.

Everyone got settled, but the noise level stayed high. "Quiet down, campers!" Hannah shouted. They paid no attention whatsoever.

Mrs. Mullins suddenly ascended from the crowd. She rose in a slow, dignified fashion, reminding Hannah of the Loch Ness monster. The former prison guard towered over the kids, casting disapproving glances on those making the most racket. The kids quieted and Mrs. Mullins sat back down.

Hannah took a deep breath and plunged in. "The first song we're going to sing tonight is 'I Want to Be a Friend of Yours.'"

Everyone groaned at the suggestion.

"You'll like it once you learn it," Hannah promised, and proceeded to sing it for them.

Then she gave the pitch and started the song. The campers' first attempt sounded like coyotes baying at the moon. In addition to singing badly, they started acting silly, as well. "Let's try that again," Hannah suggested. But neither their singing nor their behavior improved much with the second attempt.

Where was Mrs. Mullins? Why hadn't she ascended to reestablish order? Hannah glanced toward the woman's campfire blanket and noticed Harold had joined her. Mrs. Mullins batted her eyelashes at Harold and her face held a dreamy expression. Well, at least someone was enjoying her campfire.

As Jake watched Hannah try to get the campers to sing, he realized once again that she wasn't cutting it as activities director. She'd shown good sense by soliciting Mrs. Mullins's help. And it had worked, too. Until Harold showed up.

Jake sighed. He'd lived on pins and needles since the day Hannah arrived at Pine Bluff Lodge. He should have known that first afternoon that she couldn't survive camp life.

"Next, we have a relay planned by Lindy and Sara," Hannah announced.

The girls came to the front, giggling nervously. "We need twelve volunteers," Lindy announced. "And we want Mr. Reynolds and Miss Hastings to help."

Everyone clapped as Jake made his way to the front. Each year the kids found new ways to embarrass him at the campfire. What had they dreamed up this time?

Lindy faced the volunteers. "Now, this relay's real easy. All you do is form two lines and pass a grapefruit from one end of your line to the other. The trick is, you can't use your hands. You clamp the grapefruit under your chin and the next person gets real close to you and takes it with their chin. Any questions?''

Lindy and Sara proceeded to break the volunteers into two lines. Of course, they placed Hannah right next to him. Darn the kids, anyway. He'd have found it much simpler to redeem the grapefruit from one of the campers. Just the thought of getting that close to his activities director made him jittery. He considered changing places with one of the kids but before he could manage it, Lindy handed the first person on each team a grapefruit. Then Sara yelled, ''Ready, set, go!''

The race began. The agile youngsters moved the grapefruit from person to person without much difficulty. Hannah had just redeemed it from Herbert and now held the plump yellow fruit clamped between her chin and chest.

She turned to face him and her expression was unusually serious as she moved toward him. Jake leaned closer, craning his neck sideways. Then he grasped Hannah's slim shoulders—to make this acrobatic phenomenon more manageable—and leaned toward her. The feel of her soft shoulders and the fragrance of gardenias made Jake feel slightly intoxicated. He found himself a little breathless.

''Go, Mr. Reynolds,'' called one of his campers.

Hannah seemed to struggle, as well. She lost her grip on the grapefruit and it slipped a little. So Jake pressed closer, trying to keep the elusive citrus from rolling away. He managed to hold it in place, then inched it up, hoping Hannah could again secure it beneath her chin. But each time he positioned it high enough, Hannah couldn't sustain her grasp and he had to start the process all over again. It was the most exquisite torture he'd ever endured.

Jake continued his contortions and was finally able to touch the grapefruit with his chin. After several attempts, he secured a grip on it. When he finally redeemed the prize, he felt relieved to have accomplished such a difficult feat.

He pulled back and his breath came in jagged spurts—not from the challenge of the relay, but from being so deliciously close to Hannah. Then he dropped to his knees and passed the citrus to a fourth-grade girl with no trouble at all. The kids clapped wildly as Jake and Hannah's team finished just ahead of the other team.

Jake returned to his blanket, realizing that this overreacting to Hannah had to stop. When he got close to her, his pulse went haywire. And the rest of him soon followed. He couldn't go on like this. He'd always prided himself on being a disciplined man.

But even as these thoughts crossed his mind, he noticed that she looked especially pretty tonight. The orange flames created an eerie glow that reflected off her fair skin, and her silky hair shined as it swung gracefully with her movements. Her cheeks had reddened from the heat of the fire and her eyes literally danced with excitement. They always danced, making Jake's heart respond in kind.

As she waved her arms enthusiastically, directing the kids in yet another song, Jake started to mellow. While the campfire had hit a few snags, it moved smoothly now. Maybe for once he could relax.

The singing finally stopped and Jake heard a rustling sound coming from the woods. He sprang to his feet to make certain it wasn't some kind of wild animal.

It wasn't. Three figures, draped in sheets, made their way toward the campfire. Their ghostly forms emerged from the darkness. All the commotion ceased at their approach.

Was this a skit? Jake glanced at Hannah, who looked as baffled as he.

When the three ghosts reached the front, two of them shined their flashlights on a sign held by the third. The sign said, in bold, black letters:

MR. REYNOLDS LOVES MISS HASTINGS. KISSY, KISSY.

Chapter Five

"Now just a minute," Jake said, feeling a surge of annoyance and embarrassment. "This isn't funny." The campers thought it was and started to giggle.

"Quiet down, boys and girls," Hannah coached, trying regain control.

"You kids get over here this minute," Jake instructed. "I want to talk to you."

But the apparitions paid no attention. One of them reached out to throw something into the campfire, then the threesome hightailed it for the woods. Jake started after them and had only taken a few steps when an explosion of vibrant sound and color filled the air. Firecrackers! The little imps had tossed firecrackers into the campfire!

The stunning performance captured everyone's attention. Even Mrs. Mullins pulled away from Harold to see what was happening in the outside world.

Fourth-of-July sights and sounds blotted out everything else. When Jake caught his breath, he realized the kids had gotten a big head start. He'd settle up with them later.

"Campers, get back on your blankets," Hannah begged, but they were so wired from the excitement they paid no attention.

Hannah couldn't believe the scene unfolding before her eyes. Firecrackers filled the evening with resplendent color and deafening noise. Instead of directing the perfect campfire as she'd hoped, chaos again reigned.

Since there was no redeeming this out-of-control situation, she gave up and dismissed the kids to their cabins. As they ran off snickering, Hannah stared after them in disbelief. In just minutes, she and Jake were again alone.

"And you thought whoever spied on us would keep it to themselves." Jake's voice cut through the stillness that had set in the moment the kids left. A frown distorted his handsome features and a slight flush on his tanned face made him look more appealing than ever. "A sign," he said with disgust. "The little monsters announced their news to the entire camp with a sign."

"At least it was local. I'm surprised they didn't rent billboard space on Highway 71."

Jake ran his fingers through his hair and sighed. "This time Aaron isn't responsible. He's resting at his cabin and David's with him."

The flames died down and the embers now burned with a translucent glow. Somewhere an owl hooted. Its call cut through the quiet evening and sounded taunting. *If the owl could speak, what would it say?* Hannah wondered. *Probably, "Mr. Reynolds loves Miss Hastings. Kissy, kissy."*

Hannah felt totally frustrated with the campers and their pranks. She sank onto the blanket and covered her face with her hands. A moment later, Jake settled at her side. In spite of all the turmoil that characterized their relationship, she was pleased at his nearness.

"This isn't all the kids' fault," he said. "It's ours, as well. After all, we're their role models. We've got to keep our behavior exemplary. If they find a flaw in our behavior—"

Hannah jerked up her head. "A flaw? You consider kissing me a flaw in your behavior?"

"That's not what I meant. But we . . . I shouldn't have kissed you where anyone could observe."

She shrugged. "We were a mile from camp. All I saw was a couple of mallard ducks."

"We've got to remember that the kids don't miss a trick. And once a rumor starts circulating, it's murder to dispel."

Hannah sighed deeply. "So, how do we stop the rumor?"

"We starve it to death."

Hannah was growing tired of all the depressing talk of rumors and ornery kids. "Did you notice Mrs. Mullins and Harold during the campfire? At least *they* were having fun."

"A little too much fun. Did you ask Mrs. Mullins to help you maintain discipline?"

"Yes. But she got sidetracked."

"That's for sure." Jake shook his head. "As staff members, we've got to stay on task. If we don't, Camp Wildwood will turn into a zoo."

He was right, of course. But Hannah was beginning to understand Mrs. Mullins's response. She glanced over at Jake, who looked terrific this evening. A pair of jeans defined his long, muscular legs, and a forest-green T-shirt left no doubt in her mind about the strength of his upper body. She took a stabilizing breath, trying not to get as thoroughly sidetracked as Mrs. Mullins.

But it was difficult. Jake sat so close to her on the blanket that his knee rested against hers, rekindling that spark of longing she'd experienced earlier—the one that became full-blown during the grapefruit pass.

As if reading her mind, Jake said, "Leave it to the kids to choose that particular relay." He cleared his throat. "And to put us next to each other."

She laughed nervously. "I've never done the grapefruit pass before. It's pretty . . . uh, challenging, isn't it?"

When he glanced at her, Hannah sensed he was as embarrassed about the relay as she. ''To say the least.''

Being pressed against Jake in that awkward, embarrassing fashion had wakened every nerve ending in Hannah's body. She'd never thought of a grapefruit as being romantic before, but it certainly served that purpose tonight. ''I don't think I'll ever see a grapefruit in quite the same way.''

Jake smiled. ''Me, neither.''

''What did you mean about starving a rumor?'' Hannah asked, trying to stay on task as Jake had suggested.

He cleared his throat. ''We'll be especially careful. Kids tend to read things into a relationship that aren't there.''

Hannah felt a jolt of disappointment. ''Fine with me,'' she said, trying to pretend his comment didn't hurt. Obviously, the kiss hadn't meant as much to Jake as it had to her.

As he stared into the smoldering remains of the fire, his profile attractive and strong, a strand of dark hair fell across his forehead and, impulsively, Hannah reached over to push it back.

He jumped at her touch, then turned to face her, and she saw both torment and yearning in his eyes. The two emotions blended together so thoroughly that she wondered which would win.

Yearning won the standoff. Jake pulled her into his arms.

"No, Jake. The woods could be full of kids. They'll start another rumor."

"Heck with rumors," he said, burying his face in her hair.

She tried to quell the craving she had to slip her arms around him and pull him close, but the urge was too strong. Jake planted tender kisses on her face—first on her eyebrows, then her cheeks, then her chin. She must stop him. But the feelings he stirred in her heart made that particularly difficult.

Somehow she mustered up the strength to put both hands on his chest and with one frantic movement that took every once of her energy, she pushed him away. "Jake! We have to stop!"

He looked as if he'd just wakened from a dream and seemed uncertain whether to try to reenter it or face reality.

Reality won. When Jake got abruptly to his feet, Hannah felt both relief and disappointment. He reached for her hand and pulled her up beside him, and for a moment his eyes held her captive. When he turned away, she breathed a relieved sigh, uncertain if she could dissuade him a second time.

"I'll walk you to your cabin," he said quietly.

"Better not. We're trying to starve a rumor. Is it safe to leave the fire?"

"Probably. But I'll stay a while longer."

Hannah picked up her blanket and flashlight. "Good night, Jake."

"See you tomorrow," came the gruff reply.

The woods seemed darker than ever and Hannah's flashlight did little to brighten the path. But it didn't matter. The darkness fit her mood.

While her escape into Arkansas had shuttled her away from what would have been a bad marriage, she now found herself in the midst of another drama. The principal players were the ornery kids and their handsome camp director. While she was expending every ounce of energy trying to provide learning experiences for the campers, what did she get from the little ingrates? Pranks.

And she couldn't read Jake at all. Part of the time she felt certain she sensed his disapproval. At other times, she felt he was as attracted to her as she was to him.

But she didn't like what was happening between them. She wasn't in any kind of emotional shape to start another relationship when she hadn't recovered from the near-tragedy with Paul. What she needed was breathing room and a nonthreatening environment— neither of which she found at Camp Wildwood.

Hannah reminded herself again of her goal. To stay independent. Unattached. With Jake around, that proved extremely difficult.

Lightning bugs flashed Morse-code messages as Hannah made her way along the rocky path. What were they were saying? Probably "Mr. Reynolds loves Miss Hastings," like everyone else.

When she reached her cabin, she tossed the camp-fire blanket and flashlight onto her top bunk, thankful to have escaped from Jake and the monster kids. Maybe if she got a good night's sleep, things would look brighter in the morning.

A hot shower might help, too. She started collecting her toiletries when a knock at the door stopped her. She went to answer it and found a ghost waiting on her doorstep.

"Miss Hastings? Can I come in?"

Hannah pushed open the screen door. "Hurry up, Aaron. Before someone sees you."

The ghost hobbled in. "How'd you know it was me?"

"Just a lucky guess."

He limped over to one of her chairs and sat down. "What happened to you?" Hannah asked.

"I fell down when we were running away from the campfire. I twisted my ankle."

As Aaron slipped the sheet over his head, Hannah pulled over her other chair and propped his foot on it. She took his sheet, folded it, and laid it on the bunk. "It's past lights-out. Why didn't you go back to your cabin?"

"I tried to but I couldn't make it."

The child looked a sight. Poison ivy covered his body and he rubbed his now-swollen ankle. Although

Aaron hadn't been disciplined by the staff as yet, the laws of nature weren't cutting him any slack.

"Your father thinks you're with Mr. Sutton. He'll be furious when he finds out about your little prank."

Aaron's eyes pleaded. "He doesn't have to find out if you don't tell him."

"You embarrassed me at my own campfire, young man. Give me one reason why I should protect you."

"Because you're my friend."

The little con artist was pretty clever. Or was he? His compliment actually sounded sincere.

Aaron shot her another pleading glance. "We didn't mean to embarrass you, Miss Hastings. We were just kiddin' around. When we saw Dad kiss you at the Point . . ."

"So you were at the Point, too." Hannah had hoped Aaron heard about the kiss from some other camper. She should have known that wherever trouble lurked, Aaron Reynolds had a front-row seat. Blistered, itchy, and in pain, you'd think the kid would get the message that crime doesn't pay.

"Let me check your ankle. Can you pull off your shoe and sock?"

He did so, wincing in the process.

"I thought Mr. Sutton was staying with you," Hannah said.

"He was. But Mrs. Simpson got a wasp sting that started swelling so Mr. Sutton took her to the infirmary for a shot. He told me he'd be back in half an hour."

"And you sneaked out," she said with disgust. "Who were the other two ghosts?"

Aaron only hesitated a moment. "Todd and Eric."

The boy continued rubbing his swollen ankle. If he took any pleasure in tonight's performance, it didn't show.

Hannah grabbed a pillow and placed it under his ankle. "I'm going to the infirmary to get Mr. Sutton."

"Miss Hastings?"

"Yes?"

"Your cabin's really cool. It reminds me of our house when Mom was still home. She had it fixed real pretty."

Hannah reached out and smoothed Aaron's hair that had gotten mussed when he pulled off the sheet. Was that why the child was always in trouble? Because of the pain of missing his mother? "I'm glad you like my cabin, Aaron. You can visit anytime."

He grinned. "You mean it?"

"Yes, I mean it. Now, wait here until I get back with Mr. Sutton."

David checked Aaron's ankle, declaring it only a mild sprain. Then he picked up his patient to cart him back to the infirmary. Hannah breathed a relieved sigh as she watched them go.

She had an uneasy feeling that Jake might stop by while Aaron was at the cabin. Thank goodness he hadn't. It wouldn't have helped Aaron's case a bit.

Besides, she'd had enough of the two Reynolds men for one day.

After Hannah left, Jake continued to stare into the smoldering embers of the fire. He mulled over all that had happened since the fateful day that Hannah Hastings showed up at Pine Bluff Lodge. She'd literally turned his life upside down. Tonight's campfire proved another sterling example.

Tonight couldn't have been easy for her, either. The kids had publicly embarrassed them both.

Jake remembered the conversation he'd had with Hannah on their walk around the lake. She'd told him she'd planned to be married this summer, but that at the last minute, things didn't work out. Her fiancé must have dumped her. What a rotten thing to do to someone as kind and caring as Hannah. She must still be grieving over that loss. And she was also struggling to make this job work. Jake felt more sympathetic as he realized his activities director had considerable stress in her life, too.

Maybe he ought to stop by her cabin and tell her he appreciated her effort with tonight's campfire. People sometimes responded more positively to praise than to criticism.

Folding his blanket and grabbing his flashlight, Jake headed for Hannah's. He wondered if she'd changed into that incredible gown that made her look so soft and appealing. Like a woman in a perfume commercial.

Funny, that he couldn't wait to see her again when they'd parted less than an hour ago. *But only so I can give her a pep talk and help her become a better activities director,* he reminded himself.

As he approached her cabin, he noticed the light was still burning. He knocked on the door.

"Who is it?"

"Jake."

She came to the door. "I'm surprised to see you this late."

"I wanted to tell you I appreciate your efforts at campfire tonight. You worked hard."

A slight smile curved her pretty mouth. "If only it had been more successful."

"It had its moments," he said, trying to compliment Hannah while still hanging on to a shred of the truth.

"Really?"

"Really," he affirmed, hoping she wouldn't ask him what those moments were.

"Would you like a Coke?"

"You've got Coke here? It's against camp rules to keep soft drinks in the cabins."

"I know. But everyone needs a few vices—even at camp. If I had a refrigerator, I'd serve it to you cold."

"Camp Wildwood's not a high-tech place, Hannah. I explained that the day I hired you."

"I'm not complaining, Jake. I told you I could manage here and I'm doing just fine. Now do you want a Coke or not?''

He grinned. "Yes. I'd like one.''

As she went to get the soft drinks, Jake glanced around Hannah's cabin. He hadn't seen it since she'd redecorated. The bunk beds were pushed together and decked with her new lace-edged comforter and ruffled pillow shams. Curtains hung neatly at both windows.

"Your cabin looks fancy. I half expect seven little men with picks and shovels to file in singing, 'Heigh-ho, heigh-ho.' ''

Hannah shot him an exasperated glance. "Well, they'd better not. Where on earth would I put them? There's barely enough room in here for me.''

Jake chuckled as he followed Hannah to the table. She flicked open the aluminum tabs on both cans of soda and set them down.

As Jake surveyed the premises, his gaze taking in every detail, Hannah prayed he wouldn't notice Aaron's sheet folded neatly on her bed.

"So you like all these ruffles?" he asked.

"Yes, I do. Aaron likes my cabin, too.''

Jake quirked an eyebrow. "Aaron was here?''

Uh-oh. She'd almost let the secret slip. "He, um, stopped in the other day.'' The white lie made it hard for her to meet Jake's eyes.

"He did?''

"Um, yes. He said my cabin reminded him of your house before his mother left.''

Jake sighed. "Both of our lives changed radically after Rachel moved out. It's tough to be a good father and also try to fill the void his mother left. I make lots of mistakes, but I try to give my son a good life."

"I know you do," she said, well aware that Jake was a loving father.

"Do you want children, Hannah?"

"Oh, yes. I love kids. I'd hoped to start a family right away but Paul wanted to wait." She sighed. "Not that it matters now."

"Things don't always work out the way we plan." Hannah felt surprisingly comfortable talking intimately with Jake. The dim lighting in the cabin made it easier to discuss personal matters. "How long were you and Rachel married?"

"Eight years. We divorced last year when Aaron was seven."

Hannah shook her head. "That must have been painful."

He forced a smile. "Aaron and I make out pretty well on our own. Luckily I can cook. But neither of us enjoy housecleaning. Aaron plays Little League baseball and soccer, so we keep pretty busy."

"That's good," she said, sensing that in spite of Jake's comments, he felt a void in his life.

He glanced at his watch. "It's getting late. Guess I'd better head for my cabin."

Hannah couldn't let Jake leave without telling him about Aaron's campfire stunt. As she walked him to the door, she said, "Jake, I have something to tell you." She cleared her throat, stalling for time. "It's about Aaron."

Having Jake so close made this task even tougher. The strand of hair had again slipped across his forehead and she almost reached up to brush it aside, the way she had earlier in the evening. But remembering how much trouble that had caused, she resisted.

"What about Aaron?"

"He . . . he's . . . a good kid," she said, hating to tell Jake about Aaron's most recent shenanigans. It would make things even more difficult for the child.

"His behavior doesn't always back that up."

"It's just a stage. He'll outgrow it."

Jake hesitated another minute, locking his gaze on Hannah so assiduously that she felt the heat rise in her cheeks. For a moment she thought he'd reach out for her. If Jake pulled her into his arms now she didn't know if she could resist letting him kiss her.

Thankfully, he didn't. "I know your summer hasn't been easy, Hannah. With your fiancé abandoning you the way he did."

Her blue eyes widened in surprise. "Paul Arnold didn't abandon me. I left him."

"You left him? Why?"

"Because Paul wanted to run my life. He made decisions without even consulting me."

"What kind of decisions?" Jake asked, surprised by

the news that it was Hannah who'd called off the wedding.

"Everything from ordering in restaurants and choosing my clothes, to deciding what job I should take. Paul had one-year, five-year, and ten-year plans for my life I didn't realize how controlling he was until it was almost too late."

"So you broke off the engagement. I hope you let him down easy."

"There wasn't time. I told Paul I couldn't marry him just before the wedding ceremony."

Hannah noticed the change in Jake. His dark eyes clouded and his brow furrowed. "You mean you didn't give him advance notice? You left him waiting at the altar?"

Hannah squirmed under his gaze. "Well, sort of. It wasn't the best way to end a relationship, but I just couldn't marry Paul. And I didn't figure that out until the last minute."

Hannah sensed the coolness in his attitude. "What you do is your own business, Hannah. It's getting late and I'd better be going."

He left without another word. Hannah went out on her small porch to look at the moon. It hung like a golden ball in the dark sky and she imagined she could detect a face in it. It was the fabled man in the moon and he was smiling.

Personally, she didn't have much to smile about. Nothing was going right at Camp Wildwood. Her campfire had been disrupted by the appearance of the ghosts. But that didn't upset her as much as the conversation she'd just had with Jake. He'd made it perfectly clear that he disapproved of her canceling the wedding at the last minute. And his cool reaction to that news had flustered Hannah, and she forgot to tell him about Aaron's ghost prank.

She sighed. She'd have to tell him first thing in the morning.

Chapter Six

Harold handed Hannah a plate of buttermilk pancakes topped with several slices of crisp bacon. "The captain told me you're pretty handy in the kitchen. Could you help me out?"

A wave of anxiety tugged at Hannah. Another of her little white lies had come home to roost. "Sure," she said bravely. "When do you need me?"

"I've got to make a quick run to Fayetteville. My sister's sick and I'm taking her to the doctor. Could you fix supper?"

Hannah nearly dropped her plate. "You mean cook it?"

Harold grinned. "Unless you can figure out a way to get it airlifted in."

"Gee, Harold, I don't know if—"

"I'll get you some help, Hannah," he interjected. "The captain will gladly pitch in. He's a pretty decent cook himself."

Hannah shook her head. "Don't bother Jake. I'll manage on my own," she said, not the least bit interested in sharing the kitchen with Jacob Reynolds.

"The menu's all planned. Spaghetti and meatballs, Jell-O salad, French bread, and chocolate chip cookies for dessert. My recipes are easy to follow. You won't have any trouble."

Hannah forced a brave smile. "I'll do my best." She carried her tray to a table and sat down but had difficulty choking down her pancakes as she considered the prospect of cooking supper for nearly fifty people. She'd only given one dinner party in her life and that was for six friends. She'd invited them over for lasagna, green salad, and chocolate mousse.

It was a less-than-raving success. The lasagna congealed into a gummy mess. She'd ended up scraping it into the garbage disposal and making a mad dash to the local deli to buy more. She'd barely had time to spoon the substitute lasagna out of its Styrofoam container before her guests arrived. And while the green salad proved edible, the chocolate mousse wasn't light and fluffy like she'd hoped. Its texture resembled the paste her kindergartners brought to school each September. Now, it was possible to bluff your way through a dinner party for six. But preparing a meal for an entire campground?

Aaron walked by with his breakfast tray. "Morning, Miss Hastings."

"Hi, Aaron. How are you doing?"

"Better. The poison ivy's not so itchy and my ankle feels better."

"I'm glad."

Aaron joined some of his friends at a nearby table. He looked happy. Normal. Kids were pretty resilient.

But he wouldn't be quite so happy once Jake learned about his antics at the campfire. As soon as she finished breakfast, she had to tell Jake the whole sordid story. She'd put it off too long already.

Hannah finished eating and carried her tray to the dish window. She spotted Jake across the room and walked toward him, but before she could reach him, Jake blew his whistle and called the kids together for a meeting. Strange time for a meeting.

"How many of you attended last night's campfire?" he asked after the kids gathered around.

Every hand flew up.

"Then you already know what I want to discuss. Some unexpected guests paid us a visit. And while skits are fun, this skit went too far."

The room grew quiet. "I'd rather not punish the entire group when only three people are responsible. But I'll have to unless the ghosts confess. So if you were part of the prank, report to my office immediately. The rest of you are dismissed to calisthenics class."

The lodge emptied fast and Hannah decided to make a getaway herself. She'd waited too long to come clean.

"Hannah, can I see you for a minute?" Jake called when she was halfway out the door.

She came back, grudgingly, and sat beside him at the table. "What is it?"

"Did Harold ask you to cook supper tonight?"

"Yes."

He raised his eyebrows. "Can you manage?"

"Of course, I can manage," she said, wondering where to find the nearest Italian restaurant.

"If you need help, let me know."

"I will," Hannah agreed. But she couldn't decide which was more stressful: cooking dinner with Jake or cooking it without him.

He sighed. "The kids cleared out in a big hurry. It's obvious our ghosts don't plan to confess."

Hannah took a steadying breath. "Jake, I have something to confess myself. I know who the ghosts were."

His brow furrowed. "You do? When did you find out?"

"Last night."

"Did you have that information when I stopped by your cabin?"

She nodded, feeling a little like Benedict Arnold.

"And you didn't tell me? Hannah, it's essential for

the staff to stick together.'' His eyes drilled deep, stirring a mixture of fear and longing inside her.

"I tried to tell you, Jake, but we got off on other subjects."

He crossed his arms over his chest. "Which kids were responsible?" he asked.

Hannah swallowed hard. "Todd. And Eric. And . . . and . . ."

He quirked an eyebrow. "And who?"

"And Aaron."

He scowled. "That's impossible. Aaron couldn't have been involved. He was resting at his cabin."

"No, Jake. He wasn't."

Her employer's scowl intensified as he absorbed the news. He ran a hand through his hair and sighed. "Wait till I get my hands on that boy."

Hannah reached over and squeezed Jake's arm. "Jake, don't be too tough on him."

He shot her an annoyed glance. "I know how to discipline my son, Hannah."

He got up and stormed out of the lodge, letting the screen door bang shut behind him.

This time Hannah has gone too far, Jake thought as strode toward the volleyball court where Desiree held calisthenics class. Not to be upfront with him when the campers misbehaved was inexcusable.

But he knew his anger wasn't solely due to Hannah not speaking up. Much of it grew out of the fact that, once again, Aaron was in trouble.

Jake beckoned to Aaron who was preparing to exercise with the rest of the campers. His son came hurrying to his side. "What's wrong, Dad?"

"I need to talk to you. Let's go to the pier."

They walked onto the pier and Jake turned to face his mischievous son. "I know you were one of the ghosts at the campfire last night."

Aaron studied his sneakers. "You do?"

"I do. You're in trouble, young man. Big trouble. I want to see you, Todd, and Eric in my office in half an hour. Is that clear?"

"Yes, sir."

"Now, run along."

Aaron disappeared in a hurry and moments later, Hannah walked onto the pier. "I should have told you about the prank sooner, Jake. But Aaron and I really bonded last night. He came to my cabin and told me what he'd done. He felt he could trust me. And while I wanted you to know the truth, I guess part of me wanted to protect him."

"Aaron has to take responsibility for his actions. If he misbehaves, he's punished. That's the way we work. As a staff member, it's critical to the welfare of this camp that you're upfront with me, Hannah."

"I realize that. It won't happen again."

A tense silence filled the morning air. Hannah sat down on the edge of the pier, slipped off her sandals, and lowered her feet into the blue-green water of the lake. Jake watched as she submerged her feet gradually, letting her skin adapt to the cool temperature.

Sheltering her eyes from the bright sunlight, she looked up at him. ''I think you're making too much of this. It was a prank, nothing more. Not much different than the skits we have at campfires.''

Jake sat beside her. In spite of his anger, Hannah had a magnetism that drew him. The white shorts she wore showed off her tanned, shapely legs. She'd knotted her T-shirt at her waist, and even though its logo said ISLAND PARADISE, she looked a little more like a camper today than a refugee from the South Seas. ''Maybe you're overreacting,'' she said quietly.

He was overreacting, all right. But not to the ghost prank. He was overreacting to Hannah. He kept trying to squelch this runaway attraction, but it wasn't working. ''If I let all the kids get away with crazy stunts, we won't have a camp. We'll have a circus,'' he grumbled.

She sighed. ''I suppose you're right. But don't be too hard on Aaron. He's just a kid. He's going to make lots of mistakes.''

To be honest, Jake wasn't as bothered by the ghost stunt as by what happened later. Aaron had taken his secret to Hannah. Jake saw a bond forming between Hannah and his son that worried him. If Aaron got too close to her, he'd get hurt again.

As he watched Hannah move her feet through the water, creating ripples in the lake's smooth surface,

Jake realized he'd better follow his own counsel. He couldn't afford to form a strong attachment with Hannah any more than Aaron could. But it took all he had to fight it.

Her gardenia scent sweetened the air and he suppressed an urge to reach out and touch her hair that tumbled over her shoulders like liquid sunshine.

"Do you plan to punish Aaron?" she asked.

"Absolutely. No swimming for the next two days. The same goes for Todd and Eric."

While she didn't comment, Jake sensed her disapproval. But he couldn't keep getting sidetracked by Hannah. Not by her great looks. And not by her opinions about child-rearing.

Each day his feelings for Hannah grew stronger. Her smile magnetized him and her laugh warmed his heart. He found himself wanting to hold her again, to caress her silky hair, to pull her close.

He'd better keep his guard up. If he didn't, he'd be in more trouble than Aaron.

Early that afternoon, Hannah went to the lodge to get a head start on cooking supper. She glanced around the big kitchen, wondering where to begin. The room itself seemed intimidating. All the gleaming pots and pans hung neatly on pegboards, just waiting for her to make a mistake.

She decided to start with the French bread. Harold had told her it took time for the yeast to rise. After studying the recipe, she measured dry yeast into the huge mixing bowl Harold had set out. The recipe had said to add warm water to activate the yeast.

Why waste time? Surely hot water would activate it more quickly. She'd rather not spend the whole afternoon cooking if she didn't have to.

Turning on the hot-water tap, Hannah carefully measured the liquid and poured it over the yeast. Then she stirred in flour and eggs. The dough looked awfully sticky and she had considerable difficulty stirring it with her wooden spoon. She finally managed to get the ingredients blended. Now she was supposed to knead the dough. That meant putting her clean hands into that gummy mess.

Taking a deep breath, she buried her fingers in the dough and, just as she suspected, she couldn't get them back out. It took forever to scrape the mixture back into the bowl where it belonged. She'd skip the kneading process. Covering the bowl with a tea towel, Hannah prayed the dough would do its own thing.

Next, she prepared the Jell-O salad, then decided to chop onions for the meat loaf. After placing a big onion on the cutting board, she hacked it in two. The onion released a potent fragrance that burned her eyes and stung her nostrils.

Tears clouded Hannah's vision and she stopped long enough to tie a tea towel around her nose and mouth, then returned to her task. There, that helped. She chopped onions until she felt breathless from their pungent odor. The tears streaming from her eyes slowed the process.

The back door opened, then slammed shut, and Hannah turned to see who had come in. Jake stood before her, hands planted on his hips. "Are you preparing for surgery or planning to hijack an airplane?"

Hannah pulled off her tea towel and wiped her face with the back of her hand as a fresh batch of tears rolled down her cheeks. "I haven't quite decided."

Jake looked surprised. "You're crying, Hannah. Is fixing dinner too much? I told you I'd help."

"Cooking's not the problem." She sniffed. "The onions are."

He looked relieved. "That's good. How's dinner coming?"

"Just great."

"Listen, I have some free time. I'd be glad to help."

Having Jake so close made it hard to concentrate and she needed to give her full attention to her work. Being around him did strange things to her. Made her giddy. Made her legs feel like that Jell-O she'd mixed up earlier.

"What do you say, Hannah?"

"Well, it's nice of you to volunteer," she replied, trying to decide which way to jump. While Jake's offer sounded tempting, with him in the room, she'd be aware of his every move, his every gesture, his every glance.

She finally decided she couldn't afford to turn down

help in any form. Not even Jacob Reynolds's rugged, muscular form. "Maybe you could check the bread. I've never baked with yeast before."

He walked over and lifted the tea towel from the crock. "This dough hasn't risen at all. Did you put in the yeast?"

"Of course I put in the yeast." She walked toward him. "Let me see."

When Hannah looked into the bowl, she realized the sticky mass hadn't grown a fraction of an inch. If anything, it looked like it had shriveled. She sighed. "I can't imagine what went wrong."

Jake studied her critically. "Did you use tepid water?"

"What's tepid water? I used plain old water from the tap."

"Lukewarm water. The water temperature is very important in baking bread. Cold water won't activate the yeast, and hot water kills it."

Hannah's heart sank. "That's what happened. I killed the yeast. I thought if warm water was good, hot would be better. That it would work faster." She peered into the bowl again and sighed.

"It's no problem. We'll just mix up another batch."

Hannah felt both relief and disappointment. Even though cooking was not her forte, she wanted to prepare this meal without Jake's help. Obviously, that wasn't going to happen.

Hannah watched Jacob Reynolds, Camp Director,

place his finger under the tap and adjust the faucets until tepid water came out. "Come and feel the water temperature."

Hannah put her hand under the flowing stream. Even with the strong aroma of onions permeating the kitchen, she picked up a hint of Jake's aftershave. He brought the freshness of the woods inside.

Jake measured the proper amount of water, then added the yeast. "You can add the other ingredients," he instructed.

Hannah cracked in eggs and added flour, stirring the mixture thoroughly.

He nodded. "That's good. Now you knead it."

"I tried that," she said curtly. "It stuck to my hands and I could hardly get it off."

He grinned. "First, you put flour on your hands, Hannah. Like this."

As Jake coated his hands with flour, Hannah noticed how strong they appeared. His tanned fingers were long and straight, his nails immaculately groomed. He lifted the dough from the bowl and began the kneading process.

"You work the dough with your hands. Like this."

The yellow T-shirt Jake wore gave her an upfront view of his biceps that flexed as he worked the dough. He pressed the dough with his palms, flattening it, then plumped it up again and started the process over. Hannah was amazed that none of it stuck to his fingers. "Now you come and try."

She floured her hands and started pushing the dough around, pleasantly surprised that the kneading went much smoother. The dough felt squishy as she pushed at it with her fingertips.

"Do it like you mean it, Hannah." Standing behind her, Jake slipped his arms around her waist and started working the dough with his powerful hands. "Like this."

She tried to observe the mechanics of the process but the feel of his muscled body against hers sent all thoughts of bread-making skittering away. She thought about other things—like leaning against Jake and molding herself to him. His warm breath on her neck sent shivers down her spine.

Jake kneaded away, oblivious to the effect his nearness had on her. "Do you see what I'm doing?"

"Y-yes," she stammered.

As he moved rhythmically, all Hannah could think about was that if she turned around, she'd be in his arms. That thought made her even more giddy and light-headed.

Chastising herself for her errant thoughts, Hannah struggled to concentrate. But Jake continued his deft movements, making concentration impossible.

"Want to try it now?" he asked.

She nodded and her head accidentally bumped against his chest, which sent her heart off on another merry chase.

Jake took a step back and peered over her shoulder

as she tried to make her hands manipulate the dough the way his had. She felt suddenly angry about her lack of discipline and attacked the dough with a fervor.

"Much better." Jake took another step back which allowed Hannah room to breathe. But the minute he moved away, she missed his nearness. He oozed a confident strength that she admired.

When she'd thoroughly kneaded the dough, Jake scooped it up and plopped it back into the large bowl. He rinsed his hands under the faucet. "Let this rise for an hour. I've got to check on the swimming class, then I'll come back and see how it's doing. What's next?"

"Frying the meatballs and making the sauce."

"We use jars of prepared sauce. That will save you time." He opened a cupboard and set several glass jars on the counter. "Think you can manage?"

"Of course," Hannah said confidently, wanting to cook something without Jake's help or advice.

He nodded. "See you later."

With that he left her alone in the kitchen. She took a deep breath and tried to block out all thoughts of how good it felt to be with Jake. Last night, holding her during the grapefruit pass, he'd made her heart beat at dangerous speeds. And today, he'd given her his kneading demonstration. Both experiences were more pleasant than she wanted to admit.

Hannah forced herself to concentrate on the task at hand: the meatball recipe. *Let's see, you combine ground beef, chopped onions, eggs, and oatmeal, then "season to taste."* But the recipe didn't state which seasonings to use. She'd heard other teachers at school talk about how creative cooking was. This must be the creative part.

After opening several cupboard doors, Hannah finally located the one containing the spices. Basil? Alum? Cream of tartar? None of those sounded right.

She'd rather use something familiar. On the next shelf she spotted ginger and nutmeg. Those were faithful old standbys. She dumped in some of both spices, then added some cinnamon for good measure.

She rolled the ground beef into little balls, pleased when the mixture didn't stick to her fingers the way the bread dough had. Next, she poured oil into the skillet and began frying. The meatballs hung together pretty well and Hannah's confidence returned.

By the time Jake got back, the meatballs were nearly all fried and she'd filled a big pan with water to boil the spaghetti. "Have you checked on the bread?" he asked.

"I'm afraid to. If I look into that bowl and see another withered lump . . ."

"I assure you that won't happen. Come over here."

Hannah went to stand beside him as he lifted the tea towel, then peeked at the mound of dough that had risen to fill the bowl. "Wow! Pretty impressive."

He nodded. "All you have to do now is shape it into loaves, let it rise once more, then bake the bread for half an hour. If everything's under control here, I'll run into town for supplies."

"Go right ahead," Hannah encouraged, glad he was leaving so she could focus all her attention on cooking. She smiled confidently. "When you get back, I'll have dinner ready."

As Jake drove the distance to the general store, he thought about the moments he'd spent in the kitchen with Hannah. He'd enjoyed helping her, although once again he'd found it difficult to keep his attention focused.

Hannah smelled like sunshine. Her hair had brushed his face as he showed her how to knead the dough, and he almost buried his face in it and forgot all about baking. While he wasn't impulsive by nature, when he was around Hannah his brain took a backseat to his emotions.

She didn't seem to have much kitchen experience. Maybe he shouldn't have left her alone. *Don't be so paranoid,* he thought. They'd corrected the bread problem, so there wasn't anything else to go wrong, was there? A vague uneasiness nagged at him.

He drove fast, shopped in a hurry, and while picking up various items from the list Harold had prepared, he spotted a display of small coolers. Maybe he'd buy one for Hannah. That way she could get ice from the lodge and take it to her cabin. She'd have cold Coke instead of the lukewarm stuff she'd served him last night.

Funny, that lukewarm Coke tasted better than anything he'd had in ages. It wasn't so much the beverage he'd enjoyed as the company.

He thought of Hannah cooking her little heart out in the lodge kitchen. When he'd returned from swimming class, she was frying the last of the meatballs. Grease spurted in every direction, but he hadn't wanted to criticize. Thinking about it, he felt a little anxious about how dinner would turn out. He didn't want to drive the entire camp to Burger Heaven for supper.

After finishing his shopping, Jake pulled the Bronco back onto the highway and put his foot to the floor. He should have allowed more time. What if some other catastrophe had occurred?

He reached the lodge at 4:30 and dinner would be served at 5:00. As he opened the back door, he saw Hannah. At least she was in one piece and the kitchen was still standing. He breathed a relieved sigh. "How's it going?"

"Just fine," she replied, but her eyes were too bright. They looked glazed over.

"How's the Jell-O salad?"

"Came out great. It set up nice and firm." She hesitated a moment, then added, "But the bread had a serious accident."

He should have known. "What happened to the bread?"

She chewed on her lip. "Well, it came out a little dark."

"How dark?"

She picked up a loaf and showed it to him. The crust was black as pitch. "What did you set the oven on?"

"Four hundred and fifty. Just like the recipe said."

"The recipe said three hundred and fifty. An extra hundred degrees makes quite a lot of difference."

She was keeping a stiff upper lip in spite of the culinary disaster, and her stoicism tugged at his heart. But he couldn't get too sentimental. He had forty-five hungry people who'd be lining up for dinner any minute. And they wouldn't be interested in charcoal bread.

"What about the meatballs?" he asked, afraid to hear her reply.

She smiled. "They came out good. They're round and everything."

"That's nice. Meatballs should be round. And the spaghetti?"

She hesitated. "I had a little problem with the spaghetti."

Jake took out his handkerchief and mopped his brow, trying to hold the panic at bay. "What happened to the spaghetti?"

She walked over to the big pot on the stove and lifted the lid. "It all stuck together," she said. "Instead of being individual noodles the way I'd hoped, they fused together into one huge clump.''

Jake looked into the pot and sighed. He'd never seen noodles meet with such a fate. ''Pour off the water and we'll slice off chunks of it and layer meatballs and sauce over the top. You start slicing and I'll defrost some store-bought bread.''

Hannah had to admit that she was glad to see Jake. She didn't want to try to serve this meal alone. She began cutting off hunks of spaghetti, then ladling on the meatballs and sauce. Thank goodness she'd already dished up the Jell-O into small bowls, because the kids were lining up at the lodge door.

''What did you fix for dessert?'' Jake called as he laid out slices of frozen bread onto a huge tray to defrost.

''Dessert! I forgot about dessert!'' she said, thinking she'd failed miserably.

''Don't worry. We'll open up some canned peaches.''

Hannah didn't have time to worry. The kids moved to the end of the serving line where they waited expectantly. Any minute now they'd descend like hungry vultures.

She panicked. ''Jake! They're coming!''

He walked over and slipped his arm around her waist and for a brief moment, she leaned against him. The security of Jake's arm gave her the courage to face the starving campers. When he reached up to brush a strand of her hair from her face, the tender gesture made her heart flutter.

"You dish up the spaghetti and meatballs," he said, "and I'll serve the salad, bread, and the peaches."

The tender moment passed. As the kids flocked toward them, Hannah had no more time to think. Not about her struggles in the kitchen or about how good Jake's arm had felt around her waist.

"Where's Harold?" asked Todd as she handed him his dinner plate.

"He had to leave for a while."

"So who cooked dinner?"

"I did."

"Oh."

"What's that stuff under the meatballs?" Herbert inquired.

Hannah smiled. "Sliced spaghetti. It's the latest fad in Italy."

"Cool." Herbert turned back to Lindy. "We're having sliced spaghetti."

One by one, the kids filed past, taking their food and settling at the tables. After the last camper and staff member was served, Jake said, "Let's go eat. I'm starved."

He dished up two plates and Hannah followed him numbly to a table, not sure she wanted to find out what the food actually tasted like. After they sat down, she took a tentative bite of her meatball. It tasted a little like spice cake.

As Hannah watched Jake sample a meatball, she held her breath. He chewed it contemplatively. "Interesting flavor," he observed. "What spices did you use?"

"You don't want to know."

"It's not bad, Hannah. Is this your first time to cook for a large group?"

"First and last," she said firmly. Jake grinned, and his warm smile eased a little of her anxiety.

"Harold phoned," he told her. "His sister's fine and he'll be back late tonight."

"Thank goodness." Hannah finished the last bite of her sliced spaghetti. "Guess I'd better get in there and tackle those dishes."

"The Simpsons volunteered to clean up so you wouldn't have to."

"That's wonderful, I'm exhausted. Think I'll turn in early tonight."

After they said good night and Hannah stepped out into the evening air and headed for her cabin, a feeling of discouragement set in. While she'd managed to prepare a passable meal, she realized that being around Jake affected her much more strongly than it should. His nearness left her both flustered and confused.

She thought again of how close she'd come to marrying Paul. Fortunately, she'd realized her mistake just in time. The near-miss made Hannah feel troubled, and she reaffirmed her desire to stay unattached.

Besides, she couldn't afford to get involved with

another man so quickly. How would she know if her feelings for Jake were real? They might be just a rebound reaction.

But when she and Jake were together, it didn't feel like a rebound reaction. She enjoyed his company more and more. Serving dinner had been fun because she they'd done it together. If this continued, she was afraid she might fall in love with him.

Falling in love doesn't fit in with your long-range goals, she reminded herself sternly.

Even her short-range goals weren't working too well. The job wasn't going as smoothly as she'd hoped. The tasks were challenging, and having Jake around interfered with her ability to think.

She sighed. Had she taken on a responsibility that she wasn't suited for? While she was a darned good kindergarten teacher, could she cut it as activities director of Camp Wildwood?

The thought of resigning passed through her thoughts. But she didn't want to resign. She was bonding with the campers, especially Aaron, and more than anything she wanted to positively affect their lives.

Besides, if she resigned, she might never see Jake again. And the feelings she had for him, feelings she constantly fought, grew stronger each day.

She sighed. She couldn't even imagine life without Jake.

Chapter Seven

Jake knocked on Hannah's cabin door. She appeared, dressed in her gown. He swallowed hard. "I, um, bought you something at the general store."

She eyed him cautiously. "You bought something for me?" She pushed the screen door open. "Want to come in?"

Jake stepped in, handed her the bag, and watched her pull out the cooler.

"Why, thank you, Jake. But what's it for?"

Jake suddenly wished he hadn't bought the present. Why had he thought Hannah would like something as ordinary as a cooler? "It's for ice. You can fill it at the lodge and keep ice in your cabin."

"That's great." Hannah reached out to touch his shoulder and her soft touch sent an electrical charge through him. When she pulled back, his shoulder tingled where her fingers had been.

She lifted the cooler lid. "It already has ice in it. How considerate. I'll fix you a Coke, Jake. A cold one this time."

"I brought a couple of glasses from the lodge." He reached into the sack and produced them, and Hannah's eyes lit with pleasure.

"Terrific."

A warm feeling flooded Jake's chest. Hannah liked his gift, after all. He didn't think she could look much happier if he'd brought her an armload of roses.

But there's a reason for this gift, he reminded himself. His new activities director needed more supervision. Too many of her activities teetered on the brink of disaster. So far there hadn't been any serious repercussions, but what would happen if she took the campers on a canoe trip? He'd spend all afternoon fishing kids out of the lake.

She retrieved two cans of soda while he filled the glasses with ice, then poured their drinks. They settled at Hannah's table with its flowered tablecloth. "Pretty elegant," she said.

He glanced around the small room. "If you call a cabin with exposed rafters and a light bulb dangling from the ceiling elegant."

"I meant the ice. I no longer take simple pleasures for granted. Like ice cubes and air-conditioning."

Jake chuckled. He glanced at Hannah and noticed

that her hair shined like cornsilk in the dimly lighted cabin. He wondered if it felt as soft as it looked and stopped himself just before reaching out to check. Reminding himself sternly that he'd come here for a reason, he said, "We need to talk."

"Oh?"

"About your next activity. I want to help you plan it. In explicit detail," he added, knowing she wouldn't like his interfering.

Her brow furrowed. "I see. Listen, Jake, if you're dissatisfied with my work, I—"

"I didn't say that. We just need to troubleshoot ahead of time."

All the warmth he'd seen in her eyes when he'd given her the present quickly disappeared. "What do you have in mind for tomorrow?"

"A square dance. I promised the kids we'd have one."

Jake sighed. He'd hoped Hannah had forgotten about the square dance. To him, it sounded like unbridled chaos. "I'm not sure that will work. We'd need a caller and suitable music." He shrugged. "Unfortunately, we don't have either."

She flashed him a coy smile. "Well, actually we do. I had a long talk with Harold the other day. He told me all about his family, his Army career, even his hobbies. Did you know that Harold's a certified square dance caller?"

"You're kidding."

She shook her head. "Amazing, isn't it? And he even keeps a tape of hoedown music in his truck."

While the revelation surprised Jake, what amazed him even more was how quickly Hannah got close to people. She already knew more about Harold than he did after working with the man for five years.

"I don't know how well the kids would handle a square dance," he countered, still hoping to steer Hannah in a different direction.

But the disappointment in her eyes made him reconsider. He couldn't say no to all of her suggestions. Maybe a square dance could work. At least they wouldn't have any ghost appearances. "You really think you can get these kids to dance?"

She brightened. "Of course, I can. Even my kindergartners know some of the simpler steps. Our kids will shine."

Our kids. Having Hannah use that phrase about his campers touched Jake's heart. In just a few days, she seemed as dedicated to Camp Wildwood as he was.

Another thing he liked about Hannah was that she got excited about little things. Like coolers and square dances. The people he associated with, mostly clients, seemed jaded by comparison. They only got excited about court battles and big settlements. Many of them had turned callous and bitter and saw life as a battleground.

"We'll hold the dance at the lodge tomorrow at

seven o'clock," she bubbled. "All we need to do is fold up the tables. Can I borrow your tape player?"

"Sure thing."

"Harold will handle the rest. Would you like another Coke, Jake?"

"Yeah. I would."

As Hannah refilled their glasses, Jake tried to think positively about the square dance but still felt uneasy. The ideas Hannah dreamed up sounded relatively tame in their early stages, but they could spiral out of control fast.

Her first attempt at quantity cooking had made a wreck out of him. When she showed him the burnt loaves of French bread, he felt a little panicky. And when he looked into the pot and found the spaghetti had congealed into one mammoth noodle, his panic had mounted.

Remembering her now in that gown also made a wreck of him. The powerful urge to run his fingers through Hannah's shiny hair returned with overpowering intensity. Her scrubbed-clean complexion looked soft and silky, and he suppressed a desire to stroke her cheek. Or touch her shoulder the way she'd touched his earlier.

Get a grip, Reynolds, he cautioned. He'd come here to help his activities director stay focused but was getting sidetracked himself.

"So you really think this can work?"

"I'll be great. Watch and see."

"I'll take the tables down after supper tomorrow night."

"Thanks, Jake." She smiled again and when she laid her hand on his arm, his pulse started racing. "The square dance will be a great success."

He didn't know about that. All he knew was that if he wanted to remain objective, he'd better get out of Hannah's cabin in a hurry. He scooted his chair back abruptly. "Then it's settled. I'll see you tomorrow." He made a hasty retreat.

Hannah hurried up the hill to the lodge to get things ready for the square dance. Her stomach felt as if it had been dive-bombed by a colony of butterflies. She wanted this activity to be a resounding success.

Jake, Harold, and David were folding up the last of the tables as she entered the lodge. After helping them set up several rows of folding chairs, she spotted Jake's tape player on the table. "Did you bring your tape, Harold?"

"You bet." Reaching into his pocket, he retrieved it and she popped it into the machine. "Sometimes it hangs up a little. I hope it won't give you any trouble tonight."

She smiled bravely. "I'm sure it will work just fine."

When Hannah hit the PLAY button, the lodge filled with lively, toe-tapping music. She breathed a relieved sigh.

She noticed Jake out of the corner of her eye. Dressed in a turquoise Western shirt, black jeans, and a pair of black leather boots, he literally took Hannah's breath away. She hoped he wouldn't distract her from the square dance the same way he'd inhibited her cooking ability.

He came toward her. "I rigged up a microphone so the kids can hear Harold's instructions."

"Good idea."

"Anything else you need?"

There was but she hated to bring it up. He looked uncomfortable already and the dance hadn't even begun. "Have you ever square-danced?" she asked hesitantly.

"Not since sixth grade."

"I need help demonstrating the steps. Would you help me?"

His smile held a touch of cynicism. "Only if you're desperate."

"I'm desperate."

He shrugged. "Okay. I'll help."

Kids began filtering into the lodge and they broke off their conversation. Aaron, one of the first to arrive, walked over to Hannah. "Couldn't we skip this silly dance and go for a night swim?"

Hannah laid her hand on the boy's shoulder. "You'll like square-dancing once you learn how, Aaron."

"No, I won't. I'll hate it. I hate it already," he said, then went to join his friends.

"Take your seats, campers," Hannah called over the strains of "Skip to My Lou." "The staff will demonstrate some of the basic steps. Then you kids can try it."

The staff couples came forward. David and Desiree, Ron and Linda Simpson, and Mrs. Mullins and Herbert, who had learned to square-dance in school last year. When Jake came to stand beside her, Hannah felt more nervous than ever.

"First, Mr. Reynolds and I will show you how to do-si-do," she announced. "You just walk around each other, passing back to back without touching. Like this."

As they do-si-doed, Jake's tantalizing aftershave wrapped around Hannah. She reminded herself to stay on task.

Jake sighed. Hannah's mesmerizing eyes were the only reason he'd agreed to this demonstration. When he gazed into them, he felt spellbound.

She looked lovely in a white peasant blouse and a denim prairie skirt that swirled around her legs as she moved. Tonight, Hannah's clothes actually fit the occasion. She flitted past him, surrounding him with the scent of gardenias.

After they demonstrated do-si-do, she said, "Now we'll teach you how to 'swing your partner.' "

When Hannah placed her left hand on his shoulder

and slid her right hand into his, Jake noticed that it fit perfectly. As his fingers wrapped around her more slender ones, his heart was off and running. He swung her several times and the feel of her pressed against him made him glad he'd agreed to help demonstrate. When they stopped swinging, Jake felt a bit dizzy. But not from the dancing.

"And now the staff will show you how to allemande left," Hannah said.

By the time the four couples finished that step and promenaded home, Jake could have sworn the temperature in the lodge had shot up by ten degrees. He undid another button on his shirt.

Hannah turned to the kids. "All right, campers, it's your turn. We'll start out with four squares and have one staff couple in each square. Come and take your places."

"Not me," piped Aaron. "I'm not dancin' with no girl."

"Me, neither," Todd seconded.

Hannah glared at them. "Then you'll just have to sit and watch."

The girls rushed forward while the boys lagged behind, looking like prisoners on an enforced march. The staff helped the kids pair off and herded them into formation. But when Harold walked the campers through a do-si-do, they had trouble with the maneuver. "You backed into me on purpose, Eric," Lindy snapped.

"Well, get out of the way," Eric retorted.

When it came time to swing their partners, the boys did so reluctantly. "Stop huggin' me," cried a boy from another square. "Miss Hastings, tell Sara to stop huggin' me."

"No hugging, just swinging," Hannah called back.

As they attempted the basic steps, Jake tried to help Hannah keep the campers in formation. But they reminded him of a troop of monkeys. They scampered about, trying to follow instructions, but always seemed headed in the wrong direction. After walking them through all the steps, Hannah turned on the tape player. "Turkey in the Straw" blasted out at a deafening roar. For better or for worse, the square dance was underway.

Jake took Hannah's hand, bracing himself for another round of dancing with his activities director. Her cheeks had flushed to the color of a sun-ripened peach and she looked more delectable than ever. While he wouldn't admit it to anyone—scarcely to himself—he couldn't wait to take Hannah in his arms again.

"Everyone swing your partner." Harold's voice boomed over the roar of kids and music.

Jake swung Hannah round and round. She'd left her hair loose tonight and it circled her head like a golden halo. And as she pressed against him, the warm sweetness of her made his pulse accelerate.

Much as he'd like to focus his full attention on Hannah, he couldn't. The lodge teemed with noise and chaos as some campers allemanded right instead of left while others swung their corners rather than their partners, leaving kids stranded in the middle of the dance floor. Jake tried to concentrate solely on their individual square—blocking out the mass confusion, set to music, that had taken over the lodge.

He'd never seen Harold look tired but after calling a couple of sets, the man looked worn slick. "Break time," Harold announced. "Get your cookies and milk at the serving window."

He didn't have to say that twice. The kids swarmed over to get their snacks. Boys first, this time.

Hannah turned to Jake, her cheeks flushed from the dance. "How do you think they're doing?"

What could he tell her? The campers danced like a bunch of drunken sailors. About the only thing they managed to do right was stay in their own squares— most of the time. But as Hannah eyed him expectantly, Jake couldn't tell her the truth. "They're doing pretty well."

She beamed.

Fortunately, Aaron came toward them and Jake didn't have to lie again. He felt a surge of pride as his son approached. Aaron's behavior had improved over the last twenty-four hours. It seemed he was finally getting his act together. "What can I do for you, son?"

"Nothing, Dad. I need to talk to Miss Hastings."

Hannah overheard and turned to face Aaron. "What is it, Aaron?"

The boy twisted the corner of his T-shirt. "I, um, wondered if you would dance with me."

You could have knocked Jake over with a feather. Not only had Aaron volunteered to square-dance, but he wanted to dance with Hannah.

"Will you be my partner, Miss Hastings?" Aaron quizzed.

She glanced at Jake. "If your father doesn't mind."

Jake did mind. He didn't like what he saw in Aaron's eyes. It looked like puppy love. "Go ahead, son," Jake said gruffly. "I'll sit this one out."

When the music started up again, Jake sank into a folding chair and crossed his arms. If he'd thought being part of the square dance was chaotic, observing it proved more turbulent. Kids shot out in every direction, some with partners, some without. Most seemed at a total loss about where to go next. The square dance looked like a fire drill gone haywire.

In spite of the confusion, the kids were trying, Jake had to admit. Maybe this was one activity that wouldn't end in disaster. Just as the thought passed through his mind, the tape hung up. The fiddler playing "Wabash Cannonball" went berserk. The melody shot high, then dropped low, then high again.

At first, the kids looked startled. Then they began to giggle. As the music continued to lurch out of control, the giggling converted into shrieks of hysterical laughter. Finally, the music stopped all together.

Once again, pandemonium reigned. Harold went to investigate. He shook his head. "Sorry, Hannah. The tape broke."

Jake strode forward and picked up the mike. "All right, campers, settle down. Everyone take your seats."

It took a while to calm them but the laughter finally subsided. "That's better. I'm sorry we have to cut the square dance short but there are still plenty of cookies left. Mr. and Mrs. Simpson will supervise your snack. Lights-out in one hour."

Hannah couldn't wait to hand this unruly bunch over to the Simpsons. She'd seen all the children she wanted to for one day. Hoping no one would notice, she slipped out of the lodge and headed toward the pier, desperate for some peace and quiet.

While they'd been inside dancing, the weather had changed. A strong wind whipped Hannah's hair into her eyes and billowed her skirt. Dark clouds roiled on the horizon and a storm seemed imminent.

The square dance hadn't gone as smoothly as Hannah had hoped, but the kids had tried and they'd learned a few steps. What had Jake thought about the activity? she wondered. It seemed that so many of her thoughts centered on Jake and on pleasing him.

The moon was a tiny sliver of light in the darkening sky. As the wind increased, it sent waves bumping rhythmically against the pier. The threatening clouds reminded Hannah of all the turmoil in her life. Most of that turmoil centered on her relationship with Jake.

He'd looked terrific tonight in his Western shirt and jeans. His dark hair had tumbled over his forehead as he swung her to the music. If she lived to be a hundred, she'd never forget how wonderful it felt to dance with Jake. He held her close—closer than he needed to—and for those moments, she'd lost herself in the strength of his embrace. The more time she spent with him, the more trouble she had staying focused on her goal: to be independent and stay unattached.

Well, camp would end in a few days. Then she'd leave Arkansas and go home to Missouri. But Hannah knew she'd never forget Jacob Reynolds. How could she just resume her life without him?

She heard a noise and turned as a figure joined her on the pier. Jake. His aftershave sweetened the air as he approached.

She'd learned to gauge Jake's moods pretty accurately and she sensed his disapproval before he said a word. "I guess you're unhappy about the square dance," she said, beating him to the draw.

"Why do you say that?"

"Because you look so troubled."

He sighed. "I'm worried about Aaron, that's all."

"But Aaron did well tonight. I know he caused problems the first few days of camp, but he's making real progress."

"I realize that Aaron's behavior has improved."

"Doesn't that please you?"

"Yes, it does. But there's another problem."

"What's that?"

He cleared his throat. "Aaron's getting too attached to you, Hannah."

"Too attached to me? Aaron's finally interacting properly. What's wrong with that?"

"I told you about his mother," Jake said quietly. "Aaron adored Rachel. When she left, it broke his heart."

"But that has nothing to do with me," Hannah said, failing to see the parallel.

"I think it does. You've only known Aaron for a few days so it's hard for you to see how much he's changed. But he has changed. Drastically. Why, he spent half of last school year in the principal's office."

"Then you should be pleased about his progress, not upset."

When Jake reached for her hand, his warm touch made her mouth go dry. The gesture surprised her even more than this confusing conversation. "Don't you see?" he quizzed. "You're the reason for the change. Aaron adores you, Hannah. And he trusts you. I'm afraid he's beginning to count on you." He sighed. "When camp ends, you'll leave, and Aaron will be hurt again."

"So what are you saying?" Hannah demanded. "That Aaron and I shouldn't be friends? I know he's been hurt, but that doesn't mean he should never trust people again. He can't live his life without trusting.''

Suddenly, Jake reached up and stroked Hannah's hair, startling her even more. When his fingers moved to her cheek, his touch felt tender. Almost reverent. How could such a simple gesture bring forth such feeling from her?

She swallowed hard as the look in his eyes changed from concern to longing. ''Jake, I—''

He leaned toward her and cut off her words with his mouth. It claimed hers—sweetly. Gently. His kiss sent Hannah's heart racing and her emotions reeling.

She knew she should resist. Kissing Jake did not fit in with the independent life she envisioned for herself. Instead, she laced her arms around his neck.

Moving closer, Hannah gloried in the feel of Jake's arms, the taste of his lips, the wonder of him. The wind seemed to hold them together with its powerful force. And the lashing waves matched the rhythmical beating of her heart.

Hannah wanted to freeze this moment in time. Make it last forever.

A peppering of large raindrops suddenly struck her face and arms, breaking into the magic. Jake pulled away and together they gazed at the threatening sky. It rained harder and a flash of lightning zigzagged across the heavens. Reaching for her hand, Jake said, ''Come on. I'll take you home.''

They hurried toward the path leading to the cabins. As the rain beat down, Hannah almost welcomed its fury. The storm had come just in time. It had saved her from losing her perspective.

Chapter Eight

Hannah and Jake raced along as thunder hammered overhead and lightning illuminated the woods. By the time they reached her cabin, Hannah's clothes clung to her and her hair hung in dripping ringlets down her back. Jake pushed open the cabin door and she hurried inside. He followed and they both stood panting and soaking wet.

Hannah grabbed a couple of clean towels and tossed one to Jake. As they dried their faces and dripping hair, she asked. "Surely you don't think I would hurt Aaron?"

"Not on purpose, Hannah. But if he gets too attached, just the separation will hurt."

She took the damp towels and tossed them onto her top bunk. "I know life will be different for all of us when camp ends. You'll be an attorney again, rather than a camp director. I'll go back to Kansas City, look for an apartment, and prepare for another year of teaching. And Aaron will live his life, just as before."

"I hope not just as before. He got himself into a peck of trouble last year."

"Is this his first year at camp?"

"Yes."

"Maybe the camping experience is changing him. It probably has nothing to do with me."

Jake stared at her a moment, but said nothing. Then a powerful crash of thunder shook the small cabin. "I should go before the storm gets any worse."

"You can wait it out here if you like."

"No, I'd better go. Good night, Hannah."

"Good night, Jake."

The screen door slammed behind Jake as he rushed into the downpour. Hannah stared out into the blackness as rain relentlessly pounded her tiny home. As Jake disappeared into the storm, his words echoed in her thoughts. How could he think she would hurt Aaron? She already cared deeply about the little boy she'd only known a few days.

That's the problem. You're becoming much too attached, her conscience chided. She hated to think of leaving Jake and Aaron and going home.

Hannah's feelings for her new employer grew with each passing day. Their relationship had moved far beyond infatuation. On an intellectual level, she'd decided not to fall in love with Jake, but her emotions paid little attention. One touch of Jake's hand could send all her resolutions toppling.

Hannah often found herself wondering where Jake was, what he was thinking, and when she'd see him again. Her feelings for him stretched far beyond the physical. She wanted to talk with him about the campers and their problems . . . wanted to compare notes about the work they shared together.

A surge of annoyance shot through Hannah as she realized how far she'd drifted from her goal. She'd vowed to take control of her life. Both Paul and her father had been domineering men and Jake occasionally exhibited those tendencies. For once, Hannah wanted to be in charge of herself. The best way to do that was to stay unattached. But her feelings for Jake made that promise tough to keep.

The morning dawned sunny. A few branches scattered around Hannah's cabin were the only remnants of last night's storm. Taking a can of Coke out onto her small front porch, Hannah stared across the lake, noticing that dancing sun rays had turned it into a sea of diamonds. The outside world, washed clean from the battering of the storm, could begin anew in the bright sunshine.

Hannah felt a little battered herself. This push-pull reaction she had to Jake confused her. She needed a break—some time away from him. Harold would soon serve breakfast but she decided to skip it today. If she spent most of the morning in her cabin, she could avoid her handsome employer.

At 11:00 she dressed, then headed for the lodge to help Harold prepare lunch as she'd promised. He saluted when she entered the kitchen. "Reinforcements have arrived, and not a moment too soon. Potato salad for this gang is a major undertaking."

Hannah scrubbed her hands, then tied an apron around her waist. "Tell me where to start."

He pointed to a heaping pan of boiled potatoes. "Would you dice those for me?"

"Glad to," she replied, hoping dice meant to chop up into little pieces. She set to work as Harold mixed up the batter for chocolate chip cookies. "Thanks for all your help with the square dance last night, Harold."

"My pleasure. Everyone had a good time." He winked at her "You could tell by the noise level."

"Maybe not everyone."

He shot her a quizzical glance. "Uh-oh. Was the captain upset about the square dance?"

"Oh, I don't know, Harold," she said, chopping the potatoes into tiny bits and scraping them into a large aluminum bowl. Her knife flew as she took out her frustrated feelings on the innocent vegetables.

"Tell me what happened, Hannah, before you turn my spuds into mashed potatoes."

But before she had a chance to respond, the back

door burst open and Jake strode into the kitchen. Hannah nearly nicked her finger with the knife. She laid down the blade. In her hands it could be a dangerous weapon.

"Lindy fell off the retaining wall," Jake announced. "She's got a nasty bump on her head and her arm may be broken. I'm driving her to the county hospital. Will you ride along, Hannah?"

She looked questioningly at Harold.

"Go ahead, hon. I can handle the potato salad."

Hannah untied her apron. "Where's Lindy now?"

"With David," Jake answered. "I'd have him go along but I need him here on the grounds. Todd's diabetic and his blood sugar's been acting up the last few days. Besides, with thirty-five kids, you never know when the next crisis will hit."

Hannah hurried along beside Jake, trying to match her steps with his long, sure strides. She'd ended up with Jake again—even though she'd made a concentrated effort not to. Her breather was short-lived.

They reached the infirmary and one look at Lindy's tear-streaked face made Hannah glad she'd come. She hurried to the child's side. "Are you all right, honey?"

Lindy's lower lip quivered as she tried not to cry. "My arm hurts. So does my head."

David had contrived a makeshift sling for the child's arm and was applying an ice bag to the bump on her forehead. He turned to Hannah. "Don't let Lindy fall asleep on the drive over. We can't take any chances. I phoned her mother in Springdale and she'll meet you at the hospital.''

All the ominous talk pushed the little girl over the brink. Tears started streaming down her cheeks. "I want my mommy. I don't want to go to the hospital.''

Hannah knelt beside the injured camper. "Your mother will meet us there in a little while. May I ride along and keep you company?''

The child sniffed, then nodded.

"Can I carry you to the car?'' Jake offered.

Another sniff. "All right.''

Jake lifted Lindy in his arms and David relinquished the ice bag to Hannah. "Keep this on her head as much as you can.''

Hannah took the bag as she and David followed Jake out of the infirmary. Jake had already pulled his Bronco alongside the building and he helped Lindy into the backseat and Hannah climbed in beside her. David handed them several pillows which Hannah propped around the injured child.

When their seatbelts were snapped in place, Jake started the engine and drove slowly through the campgrounds, avoiding as many bumps as he could. Lindy was miserable enough and he didn't want to add to her discomfort.

Glancing into his rearview mirror, the scene he observed touched him. Hannah leaned over their small patient, her ash-blond hair gleaming in the bright rays of the morning sun. She spoke softly, assuring Lindy that the doctor could fix this and that she'd soon feel better.

Hannah would make a terrific mother, Jake suddenly realized. She had great rapport with kids. The tender expression on her face made him feel guilty about his comments of last night. He'd insinuated she might hurt Aaron. Watching her now, he realized Hannah would never intentionally hurt Aaron. Or anyone else.

His remarks had undoubtedly upset her. He figured that out when she didn't show up for breakfast.

Lindy sniffed again and Jake reached into his pocket to retrieve his handkerchief. ''Try this,'' he said, handing it back.

Lindy took the handkerchief and blew hard.

Throughout the ride, he and Hannah took turns comforting their patient. Hannah even got Lindy to giggle once or twice. Jake realized that no one else could have comforted the child as effectively as his activities director had.

He also realized that his feelings for Hannah were mushrooming out of control. He couldn't stop thinking about her. The moment he heard that Lindy'd been injured, there was only one person he wanted to have ride along to the hospital. Hannah.

More and more, he wanted talk with Hannah about the problems that surfaced with the campers. She was compassionate and forgiving. All the kids loved her. It wouldn't take much for him to fall in love with her himself. But he couldn't let that happen. His own needs couldn't take center stage. He had a son to consider.

When they reached the hospital, Jake pulled up to the emergency room entrance and gently lifted Lindy out of the Bronco. Once inside, a doctor confirmed David's suspicions. Lindy had a broken arm and a mild concussion. Just as the doctor finished applying the cast, Mrs. Jensen arrived. Lindy's delight in seeing her mother made Jake realize how lucky this little girl was. Why hadn't Aaron's mother loved him the way Mrs. Jensen obviously adored Lindy?

The woman thanked them profusely for their help and suddenly Jake and Hannah were free to go. After they got back into the Bronco and Jake started the engine, he turned to face her. "Thanks for coming along. You were a great help."

"I was just doing my job."

Her voice sounded a little formal. And polite. Too polite. "Are you hungry?" he asked, wanting to find a way to apologize. He knew he could lift her spirits with a good meal.

She sniffed. "Kind of."

"Harold's probably washed up the lunch dishes by now and it's a long time till supper. Want to get a bite before we head back? My treat?"

"Fine with me." Hannah's smile was artificial— the kind people flash when they're expected to be pleasant, but would rather not be.

"There's a diner not far from here. Nothing fancy but I hear the food's good. Want to try it?"

"Sure."

Jake turned onto Highway 71 and they drove the ten miles in silence. An awkward silence. They didn't seem like the same two people who'd laughed and chatted with Lindy all the way to the hospital.

When he pulled off the road at Willa Mae's Diner, Hannah flashed him a real smile. "I'm glad we came here. I have something to settle with Willa Mae."

Jake turned off the engine. "You know the lady?"

"She helped me find my job at Camp Wildwood."

Hannah hopped out of the Bronco and headed inside. He followed her into the diner and watched her approach a woman in a crisp pink-and-white uniform. "Hi, Willa Mae. Do you remember me? I'm Hannah Hastings."

The proprietress put down her coffeepot and gave Hannah a squeeze. "Of course, I remember you. You were my most unusually dressed customer."

Hannah flushed slightly. "I'd like you to meet Jacob Reynolds, the Director of Camp Wildwood," she said, changing the subject in an obvious hurry.

Willa Mae smiled. "So you got the job. I'm glad. Nice to meet you, Mr. Reynolds."

Jake nodded. "You, too, ma'am. I've heard lots of good things about the diner. We're looking forward to lunch."

"I'm happy to serve you. How about a booth?"

"Fine," Jake confirmed as he and Hannah followed the proprietress.

They scooted into the booth and Willa Mae handed them menus. "The special's ham and beans. It comes with cornbread, a tossed salad, and dessert."

Hannah glanced over at Jake as he studied the menu realizing again that her efforts to stay away from him hadn't panned out. The trip to the hospital went reasonably well because Lindy required their complete attention. But from the moment they left the child in her mother's care, Hannah'd felt ill at ease in Jake's company. She didn't like his implications that she would hurt Aaron.

He scanned the menu. "What sounds good?"

Everything sounded good. But after the disastrous meal at Burger Heaven, she'd determined never to overeat in front of Jake again. "I'll have the special," she said, knowing the portions would be smaller.

Jake closed his menu as Willa Mae came to take their orders. "Two specials, please."

The proprietress nodded. "Good choice." She hurried away to the kitchen.

As Jake studied Hannah, the steadiness of his gaze made her wriggle uncomfortably. "What did Willa Mae mean about your being her most unusually dressed customer?"

Hannah wriggled some more. She didn't want to discuss her canceled wedding with Jake. Just sitting across from him in the same booth she'd occupied the morning she'd run away, was painful enough. "I won't bore you with the details," she said, hoping he'd drop the subject.

Of course, he didn't. He leaned forward eagerly. "You're blushing, Hannah. Come on. Tell me."

She shot him an annoyed glance. "I'd rather not."

"Then let me guess. Let's see, did you come here in a bikini?"

She sighed. "No, Jake. I didn't come here in a bikini."

"A nightgown? That incredible one you wore the other night when I stopped by your cabin?" He leaned even closer. "Hannah, tell me you didn't come to the diner dressed in that nightgown."

She felt her face flush. "I'm not crazy, Jake. I don't run around town in my nightgown."

He lifted his glass of water and took a sip but his eyes never left her face. "What then? You've piqued my curiosity."

No way would he let this pass. She might as well confess and get this interrogation over with. "I came here in my wedding gown. Now are you satisfied?"

There, it was out. Let him laugh, or criticize, or analyze. At least he'd quit asking questions. Or would he?

He set his glass down. "Now let me get this straight. You came to a diner dressed in your wedding gown?"

Unfortunately, Willa Mae had just returned with

their salads and she overheard Jake's comment. "I don't mind telling you, Mr. Reynolds, that Hannah was a sight to behold. She looked gorgeous in that satin gown. It was princess-style with a chapel train. When she slid into this booth, I kept waiting for the groom to join her. But he never came."

Hannah wished Willa Mae would stop giving Jake more ammunition. Was nothing sacred? "May I have some coffee, please?" she asked pointedly, hoping to divert the proprietress's attention to more practical matters.

"You bet, Sugar. Coming up."

Jake eyed her skeptically, his expression a mixture of fascination and disbelief. "I can't believe you drove all the way to Arkansas in a wedding gown. Wasn't it uncomfortable?"

"Look, Jake, there was no place to change, all right?" She realized the pitch of her voice was rising but she couldn't seem to control it. When he reached over and covered her hand with his, her overtaxed nerves threatened to mutiny.

"Whoa, Hannah, whoa. I'm not criticizing. I'm just curious."

He stroked her fingers gently, stirring up a host of feelings, making her more anxious than ever. "You've got to relax," he chided, not realizing that he was the reason she was unable to.

"Listen, Hannah, if I upset you last night, I'm sorry," Jake said, abruptly changing the subject.

"Maybe I'm too overprotective of Aaron. I just want to help him get his life back on track."

She leaned closer. "I understand that, Jake. But you can't put your son in a box. He needs to form friendships. Not just with kids—with adults, too. With other adults besides his father. Who knows, maybe you'll marry again someday. If Aaron's never even been friendly with another woman, how will he accept one as a mother?"

At that moment, Willa Mae brought their meals, interrupting their discussion. After she set down their plates, Hannah and Jake ate a while in silence.

Then he glanced over and said, "I've hardly even dated in the past year. I think it will be easier on Aaron if I stay unattached. After all, his welfare comes first." Jake cleared his throat. "Not that it's been much of a sacrifice not to date until . . ." He stopped mid-sentence.

Hannah looked up and caught his gaze. Jake cleared his throat again. "Until I met you."

His words caught her off guard. "Oh," she said, feeling a shiver of delight. "So . . . so I've made you reconsider your stance on dating?" she stammered, not knowing what to say.

"You've made me realize how much I miss having someone special in my life."

Her heart skipped out of control. "I see," she mumbled.

Jake laid his fork down and reached for her hand.

"Being around you has confused me, Hannah. Big time."

"Now that's reassuring," she said, starting to get a little annoyed.

"What I mean is, and I know I'm not saying this very well, but you're helping me see that I don't want to live the rest of my life single. I honestly thought I could. But being around you has changed that."

It was starting to sound a tad more romantic. But she didn't want to be the vehicle that led Jake to other women. She wanted to be *that special someone* he wanted. *The only one.*

Of course, that went against the goal she'd set for herself.

"You've made me realize I can love again," he said softly. "I didn't think that was possible."

Hannah continued to study him, her heart pounding. What was Jake saying? That he loved her? Or just that he again felt able to love again?

Willa Mae freshened their coffee, interrupting what may have been the single biggest moment in Hannah's life.

They ate in silence. Try as she would, Hannah couldn't keep her mind off Jake and what he'd just said. Or almost said.

Willa Mae came to clear away their dishes. "How about a piece of pie? I've got apple, cherry, and banana cream."

Dessert sounded tempting. "I'll have banana cream," Hannah replied.

"And you, Mr. Reynolds?"

Jake hesitated. Surely he'd have dessert. It came with the meal.

"Just more coffee, thanks."

Hannah's heart sank. Once again she'd be engaged in an eat-athon while her employer sat by observing. She remembered the fateful trip to Burger Heaven where she'd eaten everything in sight while Jake had disciplined himself to a fault. Looked like history was about to repeat itself.

Willa Mae returned with a huge piece of banana cream pie. "How about splitting this with me, Jake?" she begged.

Thankfully, he nodded.

"I'll ask Willa Mae for another plate," she said.

"We don't need another plate. We'll share this one."

They started picking away at the pie from both sides of the table. There was something pleasant in sharing a piece of pie.

"Are you still glad you canceled the wedding?" Jake asked, bringing up marriage again.

"Absolutely."

His eyes held hers across the table. "No regrets?"

"None. Paul wasn't the man for me. I can't believe I didn't see it sooner. After our honeymoon, we would have moved into Paul's house that he'd furnished according to his taste. Danish modern. I hate Danish modern.'' She sighed. ''If I'd stayed with Paul, I'd have lost my identity.''

''Then you were wise to recognize the problem before you married him.''

IIis comment took her back. Jake's validation felt good.

''I've been thinking about what you said the other day,'' he admitted. ''About if the right two people get together, their marriage could not only work out, but be happy.''

''You disagreed with me then.''

''I know,'' he said, reaching over for another bite of pie. ''I've gotten pretty jaded handling so many divorces and going through one myself. But I've reconsidered. I think you're probably right.''

Hannah's heart picked up its pace. Was there a chance Jake felt about her the way she felt about him? Could they possibly have a future together?

IIe glanced at his watch. ''We'd better get back to camp. Oh, I forgot to mention that Friday is Parents' Day. Would you plan some sort of a reception in the morning? And maybe some games for the afternoon?''

''No problem,'' she agreed, glad to return to a more neutral topic. And also glad that her job was still in tact. ''I'll meet you at the car in a minute, Jake. I want to talk to Willa Mae.''

Hannah let him pay the bill before approaching the counter.

"Looks like you've found yourself a keeper this time, honey," Willa Mae said after Jake headed for the parking lot.

"It's not like that. Jake and I are just coworkers. And friends, of course."

Willa Mae raised her eyebrows. "I saw the way he looked at you, Hannah. It wasn't a 'just friends' kind of thing."

"Have you forgotten? Just last week I came in here devastated because I'd almost married the wrong man. I plan to stay single, Willa Mae. Permanently."

"Say what you like, Hannah, but I'm a pretty good judge of people. I watch them every day as they come to the diner. The couples who eat their meals without conversation don't usually stay together. But couples who talk to each other—really talk—do just great. You and Jake had a lively conversation going."

"And that means we should get married?"

"You protest too much, Hannah. I like your camp director. And unless I miss my guess, so do you."

Hannah felt her cheeks flush. "Better not try fortune-telling, Willa Mae. Stick to the restaurant business. Oh, I almost forgot. This is for you." She tucked an envelope in the proprietress's pocket.

Willa Mae whipped it out. "I hope this doesn't contain money."

"I'm just paying back what you loaned me."

The older woman thrust the envelope back into

Hannah's hand. "That was a gift. Now you take this and skedaddle before I get angry."

Hannah gave in. "Thank you very much. If there's ever anything I can do . . ."

"There is one thing."

"Name it."

Willa Mae winked at her. "Invite me to the wedding."

Chapter Nine

For once, the lodge was quiet. As Hannah arranged a basket of wildflowers for the reception table, she basked in the silence, knowing it wouldn't last long.

Everything was ready for their visitors. The long tables had been set up and covered with paper table-cloths, and Hannah had put bouquets of sweet william in the center of each table. While the lodge didn't come equipped with vases, drinking glasses served the purpose.

As she put the final touches on her centerpiece, the screen door banged shut. "Hi, Miss Hastings."

"Hello, Aaron."

"What are you doing?"

"Getting ready for the Parents' Day reception."

"Can I help?"

Hannah hesitated, remembering Jake's cautioning words at the pier. But as Aaron gazed at her expectantly, she didn't have the heart to refuse. "Would you fold these napkins, please?"

He grinned. "Sure."

When the screen door banged again and Jake entered, Hannah caught her breath. A pale-yellow oxford shirt accented the breadth of his shoulders, and his tailored charcoal slacks looked totally terrific. While Jake always looked great, the dressy clothes made him more appealing than ever. He strode over to the table where she was working. "What have you planned for this afternoon, Hannah?"

"A couple of relays. They should work well for both kids and adults. Maybe you and Aaron can participate."

"Don't count on us. It's hard to be Camp Director and a parent at the same time."

The sound of tires in the gravel parking lot announced the arrival of their guests and Jake went to the door to greet them. As the campers helped their folks find seats, then served them cinnamon rolls and juice, the lodge again teemed with noisy confusion.

Aaron stood by watching. "Dad's too busy to eat with me."

The child's disappointment tugged at Hannah's heart. While she wanted to make him feel better, she couldn't keep opposing his father.

Several minutes passed and Aaron looked more dejected than ever. When Hannah could no longer ignore his discomfort, she said, "Maybe we could have a cinnamon roll together."

He brightened. "Okay. I'll get us some."

While Aaron hurried off to get their food, Hannah sat down to wait, trying to dispel the feeling of guilt at again going against Jake's wishes. They'd had a good talk about Aaron at Willa Mae's Diner but that didn't mean Jake had changed his mind. As she watched him mingle and chat with the parents, she hoped he'd be too busy to notice she was spending time with Aaron.

As Todd Taylor's mother droned on and on about her son's problems in school, Jake's mind started to wander. He'd felt troubled when he entered the lodge and found Aaron helping Hannah prepare for the reception. His son's attachment to his activities director was growing big-time. Aaron looked at her with adoration. Pure adoration. He sighed, knowing trouble lay ahead. When camp ended, Aaron would be hurt again.

He'd couldn't afford to forget how dejected his son became after Rachel left. Those were the worst days of Aaron's life. And while Jake struggled himself, the hardest thing about the divorce was the pain it caused Aaron.

There was no denying that Hannah had a powerful effect on them both. Having her around made Jake realize what an empty shell his personal life had become. She made him want more from life. Love. And marriage. The whole nine yards.

And the only woman he could picture playing the role of wife and mother was Hannah Hastings. The thought that they'd soon go their separate ways hurt him deeply.

If he had only himself to think about, he'd pursue Hannah with every ounce of energy he had. If he wasn't already in love with her, he was coming dangerously close. But he couldn't just think about himself. He must consider Aaron.

Besides, he didn't know if Hannah felt the same way about him. Even if she did, would she stay with him? There was only one kind of marriage he was interested in. The forever kind. And Hannah had left her bridegroom at the altar.

As Mrs Taylor chattered away, Jake wished he could escape the talkative woman and have a snack with his child like all the other parents were doing.

Aaron was probably lonely. When Jake glanced around the room and spotted his son sitting with Hannah, his irritation peaked. "Would you excuse me a moment, Mrs. Taylor? I have some business to attend to."

He left Mrs. Taylor mid-sentence and strode over to the table where Aaron sat laughing and talking with Hannah. "Would you mind mingling with the parents for a while, Hannah? That way I can enjoy a cinnamon roll with my son." He hit hard on the words *my son*.

Hannah looked startled. Her cheeks flushed bright red. "I'd be glad to."

"No," Aaron snapped. "I don't want her to go. I want the three of us to eat together."

"That's impossible," Jake said, knowing his voice sounded cool. "We need a host or hostess to mingle with our guests. We can't leave them on their own."

He turned to Hannah, knowing he was acting like a jerk but somehow unable to stop himself. "I realize this doesn't quite fit your job description, Miss Hastings, but would you play hostess for a little while?"

"Da-a-a-a-d."

Jake leveled a threatening glance at Aaron. "That will do, young man."

Hannah flashed him an artificial smile. "I'd be glad to help make the parents feel welcome, Mr. Reynolds. After all, that's what I'm here for." She gave Aaron a genuine smile, then she turned, straightened her shoulders, and moved into the midst of the congregating parents. Soon she was talking with Susan's mother, making the extremely shy woman feel very much at home.

Jake felt like a cad. He'd just dismissed Hannah. Told her, in essence, that she didn't belong in their family of two. Why had he been so rude?

The truth was he was terrified to open up and let her into his life. If he wasn't careful, his fears would cost him the woman he loved. His pulse started pounding as he suddenly realized that he did love Hannah. He loved her with all his heart and soul.

"So, Aaron, what do you think of the reception?" Jake asked.

"Okay, I guess," Aaron mumbled.

"Harold makes the best cinnamon rolls. Don't you think?"

"Uh-huh."

But try as he would, Jake couldn't pull his son into the conversation. Aaron wasn't the chatty, friendly kid he'd been with Hannah.

"You don't seem very happy today," Jake observed.

"I wanted Miss Hastings to sit with us, Dad."

"Why, Aaron?"

"Because when she's around, we seem like a family. A real family."

His son's comment confirmed Jake's worst fears. The irritation he'd felt earlier converted to anger. "Now, listen to me, Aaron. We're not a family. Hannah and I only work together. We're friends—nothing more."

Aaron shot Jake a cool glance. "I'm sorry you don't like Miss Hastings, Dad, but I like her a lot. And I'm going to go find her right now." He scooted his chair back and left Jake sitting alone, staring at the cinnamon roll he hadn't even tasted.

Things were worse than he'd imagined. Hannah had stolen both their hearts. Jake sighed. He couldn't risk marriage a second time. What if it failed? What would that do to Aaron? What would it do to him?

Hannah hurried down to the lake, needing a few minutes to compose herself. The incident with Jake left her shaken. He couldn't have made his feelings more clear if he'd drawn her a map.

She didn't want to return to the lodge full of parents till she stopped shaking. Kneeling on the bank, she cupped her hands in the lake water and splashed some onto her face. It cooled the heat in her cheeks and startled her back to reality.

She gazed across the lake, hoping the serene landscape would ease some of her anxiety. When she'd set out for Camp Wildwood with Willa Mae's instructions clutched in her hand, she'd hoped this place would offer a new beginning. She'd hoped to put the pain of her aborted wedding behind her.

But she hadn't found any answers here. Working for Jake, and falling in love with him, had only created more problems. Bigger problems.

Camp ended in three days. The kids and staff would go their separate ways and another group would occupy the grounds. She'd have to hang on until then.

Maybe she could manage if she took Jake's advice. She would stay away from Aaron. And she would avoid his father, as well.

Just three more days. Then she'd pack her things and drive back to Kansas City. She'd look for a new apartment and find a job to keep herself occupied till school started this fall. And she'd forget all about Jacob Reynolds and his son and the profound effect they'd had on her life.

That afternoon, the lodge bulged with kids and parents. Hannah surveyed the lively crowd, fervently hoping her relays would go over well.

While this morning's encounter with Jake had upset her terribly, it hadn't seemed to trouble him. He stood before the group looking like self-confidence personified. Not a single black hair was out of place.

After Jake introduced her, Hannah came forward to give instructions for the relays. "We're pleased to have all you parents on the grounds today. Until now, you've only been spectators. But that's about to change."

The audience chuckled and Hannah relaxed a little. "Our first relay will be a three-legged race. If you'll pick up a piece of twine from the table and follow me outdoors, we'll get started."

The noisy assembly of adults and kids exited the building and followed Hannah to a grassy clearing where she divided them into teams A, B, C, and D. After each parent's leg was secured to their child's, Hannah blew the whistle and the participants started their jagged journeys across the field, hopping along like a bunch of dysfunctional bunny rabbits.

She looked around for Jake but couldn't locate him

in the melee. Surely he wouldn't leave her alone with this mob of people. Up until now he'd hardly trusted her with the campers, let alone their parents.

A moment later she spotted him. He and Aaron were at the end of Team A's line. They obviously planned to run the race. That surprised her, knowing how hard it was for Jake to serve as both administrator and parent.

Hannah watched kids and parents make their way across the grassy field. The warm summer sun seemed to smile down on the gathering. Father-and-daughter teams, mother-and-son duos—these were all people who belonged together in family units. At that moment, Susan and her dad crossed the finish line, and Susan's mother greeted them with hugs and praise. While Hannah certainly didn't begrudge these people their happiness, she felt a touch of envy at the happy interaction.

When the Reynolds family's turn came, Aaron's eyes danced with delight and Jake's grin was positively boyish. The two of them set out, moving along quickly and efficiently. Hannah held her breath as they shot ahead of the other participants and neared the finish line. If Jake and Aaron reached it first, they'd bring their team to victory.

But Sara and her father were rapidly gaining. If they passed Jake and Aaron, Team B would win the relay. Then at the last moment, the Reynolds family moved ahead, crossing the finish line to take first place. The crowd roared. And Hannah cheered the father-and-son team that had come to mean the world to her.

She now knew without a doubt that she'd fallen in love with Jake. She couldn't pinpoint the exact moment it happened, only that it had. As she watched Jake and Aaron embrace, she suddenly realized that the two of them were a complete family unit. They'd gotten over a hurdle in their lives and had learned to work together. And they obviously didn't need her. With the exception of the one afternoon at the diner, Jake had been outspoken about his future plans. He intended to stay single and to raise Aaron by himself.

It was Jake's call, she realized. She'd been a fool to think he might change his mind. She sighed, feeling lonelier than she'd felt in her entire life.

Hannah grabbed a string of suckers she'd purchased at the general store and began distributing them to the winning team. As she handed a sucker to Aaron, then to Jake, she avoided meeting their eyes. "Good job, everyone," she said, trying to keep her emotions from showing.

Then Harold appeared with a sack of potatoes and Hannah had to organize this boisterous crowd for the potato relay. "Everyone listen to the instructions," she called over the racket. "For our next relay, you'll each carry a potato across the field on a teaspoon. If you drop your potato, you may pick it up and place it back on the spoon. The first team with all its members across the finish line wins."

She blew the whistle again and parents and kids set out on their appointed task. Balancing large potatoes on small eating utensils proved a tough assignment. Potatoes rained to the ground and after replacing them on their spoons, the participants continued their jerky paths across the field.

When the relay ended, Hannah announced the winners, then everyone headed to the lodge for lemonade. Hannah watched them go, thankful that her Parents' Day responsibilities were finally over. Within an hour, the visitors would leave the grounds to return to their homes.

She hurried toward her cabin, anxious to be alone. As she entered the tiny cottage, it suddenly looked ridiculous. All the decorating in the world hadn't changed a thing. The accessories seemed totally out of place—as mismatched to the small log cabin as she was to Camp Wildwood. And to Jake.

She sank onto one of her chairs, feeling discouraged and hopeless. That first evening when she'd decorated her cabin, she had high hopes this job could work. She'd wanted desperately to fit in and become a productive staff member.

In recent days she'd thought perhaps her plan was working. She'd been more successful in her role as activities director. And she thought she'd made some strides in her relationship with Jake, as well.

At certain moments she'd even thought—hoped— that she and Jake might have a future together. But this morning when he so coolly dismissed her, reaffirming that she had no place in Aaron's life, she'd finally gotten the message. That was Jake's way of saying she had no place in his life, either.

She sighed. It was just as well. Loving Jake didn't fit into her game plan. How could she have drifted so far off course? She didn't belong in the activities director position. And she certainly didn't belong with Jacob Reynolds. She had to leave Camp Wildwood— and the complications it had added to her life—and move on.

Dragging a chair over to the window, Hannah yanked down her ruffled curtains. Next, she whisked off the flowered tablecloth, then stripped the bed. She'd deluded herself long enough.

Tears rolled down her cheeks but she brushed them aside. She couldn't spend another night in this silly little house. She couldn't spend another day with Jake and Aaron, loving them but knowing she'd never share their lives. After pulling her suitcase from under the bed, she started packing. It was time to go.

She dug a piece of scrap paper out of her purse and scribbled a brief note.

Jake:
This hasn't worked from the beginning. I was the wrong person for the job. Thanks, anyway.
                                                            Hannah

While the note referred to her job, she felt a much more profound sense of loss that her relationship with Jake had crumbled. She would carry that pain with her for the rest of her life.

At 5:00 P.M., Hannah finished packing and loaded the last of her things into the Mustang. Then she started the engine and drove slowly around the periphery of Lake Wildwood toward the camp entrance. Everyone would be too busy with dinner to notice her leaving. As she turned onto the dirt road that led off camp property, loneliness engulfed her. Trying to ignore it, she stepped down on the accelerator, leaving clouds of red Arkansas dust behind.

Jake took the last bite of his dinner, knowing he needed to straighten things out with Hannah. He'd been downright rude to her this morning. That was inexcusable.

"Aaron, you've hardly eaten a thing. I thought meatloaf was your favorite."

Aaron toyed with his mashed potatoes and smeared gravy around on his plate. "I'm not hungry."

"What's wrong?"

"I think Miss Hastings is mad at us."

"She may be upset with me, Aaron, but I'm sure she isn't mad at you."

Aaron sighed. "I kind of miss her."

"Well, I kind of miss her, too. Why don't you finish

your dinner and we'll pay Miss Hastings a visit. You can even pick her some wildflowers.''

"You mean it?''

''I mean it.''

Aaron's plate was clean in no time and the two of them went to pick a wildflower bouquet. Then they walked toward Hannah's cabin. A pair of mallard ducks flew overhead, reminding Jake of the evening he'd spent with Hannah at the Point. That night was the first time he'd held her. She'd felt like heaven in his arms and her mouth tasted as satiny sweet as he'd known it would. He'd felt more alive in those moments than he'd felt in years.

"There's a taffy pull tonight, Aaron. After you say hello and give Miss Hastings your flowers, you can head over to the lodge for a while.''

"Why? Do you want to talk to Miss Hastings alone?''

"Well, sort of.''

"To tell her you're sorry about this morning?''

The kid didn't miss a trick. "Actually, yes. So you'll go to the taffy pull?''

Aaron gave Jake a conspiratorial smile. "Okay, Dad. I'll go to the taffy pull.''

Jake was dying to get Hannah alone. He wanted to apologize. Properly. That wasn't possible with Aaron tagging along. He increased his pace and Aaron had to skip to keep up.

When they reached her cabin, Jake knocked on the door. No answer. "Looks like she's not home."

Before Jake could stop him, Aaron opened the screen door and bounded inside. "She's gone, Dad! Miss Hastings is gone!"

"She probably just went for a walk."

"If she did, she took her curtains with her!"

Jake yanked the door open and hurried inside. The cabin was empty! He felt numb as he gazed around the deserted little house that Hannah had claimed as her own.

The table where they'd shared their Cokes had been stripped of its brightly flowered cloth. And the bunks Hannah had decked with frilly comforters now held only the bare, torn mattresses. Jake felt a stab of pain at the stark emptiness of the place that only hours ago had been so homey. With all Hannah's touches removed, it was devoid of all interest. All life.

Aaron laid the wildflowers on Hannah's table. When Jake saw the pain in his son's eyes, his numbness converted to anger. "Hannah ran away," he said, hardly able to control his conflicting emotions. "She ran away."

Aaron's eyes clouded with tears and he swiped at them with the back of his hand. "Will you find her, Dad?"

"I don't know, son. You head over to the lodge while I figure out what to do. Okay?"

Aaron nodded solemnly and went out, letting the screen door slam behind him.

Jake sank into one of the aqua kitchen chairs where he and Hannah had shared their Cokes and buried his face in his hands. Hannah was gone. Really gone. Shock, anger, and disappointment raged inside him.

He must have sat there half an hour trying to absorb the horrendous impact of her leaving. Finally, he started back around the lake to find Aaron. He had to make his son understand the painful truth—that they couldn't depend on Hannah. When things got tough, rather than resolve the difficulty, Hannah ran away. Only a few days ago, she'd left her fiancé at the altar. And now she'd run away from Camp Wildwood, breaking Aaron's heart.

What about his own heart? Although he'd told Aaron that he and Hannah were just friends, they'd progressed far beyond friendship. He loved Hannah. But she'd deserted them—just like Rachel.

A wave of pain washed over Jake as the full impact of Hannah's leaving struck him. It wasn't Aaron who'd have the most difficulty healing. Aaron would adapt.

But for Jake, this was a life-changing event. The woman he loved was gone. He wasn't sure he'd ever recover.

Chapter Ten

Hannah felt a little guilty as she drove past Willa Mae's Diner. While she wanted to say good-bye to her friend, she didn't feel like answering questions about Jake or her change in plans. And Willa Mae always asked questions.

But after traveling on for short distance, Hannah changed her mind. Willa Mae had been there when she needed her. She turned the Mustang around and drove back to the diner.

She found the proprietress sitting in a booth, painting her fingernails. Her pink-and-white uniform had been replaced by black slacks and a turquoise silk blouse. "Hi, Willa Mae. You look terrific."

The woman glanced up from her task. "Hannah! How nice to see you again."

"Aren't you working tonight?"

"I've got a date, so Sandy's covering for me. But I have time for coffee. Sit down."

Hannah slid into the booth and Sandy set down two steaming mugs. "Tell me the latest," Willa Mae prompted. "How are things between you and your handsome camp director?"

Hannah sighed. "Awful. I've left Camp Wildwood and I'm heading back to Kansas City. I just stopped in to say good-bye."

Willa Mae tightened the lid on the nail polish and studied her with dismay. "What went wrong, child? When you and Jake came here for lunch things seemed to be going so well."

Hannah told her friend the whole, sad story—all the way back to Rachel's leaving and what that did to Aaron. "Jake doesn't want another relationship," Hannah explained. "And he's extremely protective of Aaron."

"They've both been hurt. It's natural that Jake would be cautious." Willa Mae reached over and patted Hannah's hand. "What a shame. I sensed a chemistry between the two of you. But I suppose you'll sit there and deny it."

Hannah shook her head. "The chemistry was there. And it went beyond chemistry. I've fallen in love with Jake."

Willa Mae smacked her hand down on the table. "And I'd bet my diner that it's mutual. What did Jake say when you told him you were leaving? Did he ask you to stay?''

''I . . . I didn't exactly tell him.''

''You didn't exactly tell him? What does that mean? You used sign language?''

''I . . . I left a note.''

''A note? Tell me you're kidding!''

Hannah sighed. ''Talking to Jake wouldn't have done any good.''

''Well, what about Aaron? Imagine how hurt that child will be when he finds out you've gone.''

The words struck a nerve. Hannah'd been so busy thinking about her own pain, she hadn't given enough thought to Aaron's. ''I know he'll be disappointed and I hate to add to his problems. Aaron was a pistol when camp started, but he's shaping up. He's much better behaved now.''

''Maybe that's due to your influence. Looks like you've stolen Jake's son's heart, as well.''

Hannah sipped her coffee. ''You've got it all wrong, Willa Mae. As a divorce attorney, Jake sees the messes people make of their lives. He has no intention of marrying again. He told me so several times.''

''Shoot, Hannah. You can't believe everything people say. You probably made him nervous. While he didn't intend to fall in love with you, he—''

''You're reading things in that aren't there.'' Hannah sighed. ''Well, it doesn't matter now. With everything that's happened, I couldn't stay on at Camp Wildwood.''

"So you just up and left without an explanation.''

"What could I say? 'I'm really sorry I didn't meet your expectations as activities director?' ''

"Is that the real issue here?''

Hannah rubbed her temples. "Oh, I don't know. I'm so confused.''

"Try to put the problem into words. Tell me just like you would tell Jake.''

Hannah took a steadying breath. "Okay. I'd say, 'Jake I've fallen in love with you. Hopelessly and passionately in love with you. But, of course, this doesn't fit in with my plans to be an independent woman.' ''

Willa Mae nodded. "Go on.''

Hannah took an even deeper breath. '' 'I think there's a chance you love me, too. But a wife and a new mother for Aaron aren't part of your game plan. So that leaves us totally stymied.' ''

"Very good. Now go back to Camp Wildwood and say that to Jake. In exactly the same words.''

"And then what?''

"Then the two of you will work out solutions to your problems together.''

Sandy came by and topped Hannah's coffee. "Willy, your fella just pulled in.''

"Tell him I'll be out in a minute.'' Willa Mae stood and smoothed her slacks. "You're special, Hannah. You deserve a good life. Don't cheat yourself out of happiness by not facing problems while they can still be solved.'' She leaned down and gave Hannah a quick squeeze. "So long, Sugar. I wish you the best.''

After Willa Mae had gone, the heavy discouragement returned. Hannah felt as if her heart had been torn into a million tiny pieces and stomped on by an elephant herd. A profound loneliness flooded her as she realized she might never see Jake or Aaron again.

"Can I get you something else?'' Sandy asked.

Hannah suddenly decided to eat herself into oblivion. "Yes, please. A hamburger, a double order of fries, and a chocolate malt.'' But when the food came, she only took a few bites before pushing the plate aside. This time, her problems were too big to fix with fat grams.

She went to the counter to pay Sandy. "I couldn't help overhearing your conversation with Willa Mae,'' the waitress said. "What are you going to do? Try to patch things up with Mr. Reynolds? Or go back to Kansas City?''

Hannah shrugged. "I wish I knew.''

Out in the parking lot, she slid into the Mustang, started the engine, and shifted into gear. As she approached the highway, she couldn't decide which blinker to turn on. Left would take her back to Kansas City. Right, to Camp Wildwood. And Jake.

The night she'd almost married Paul suddenly flashed before her in bold relief. That had been a crossroads in her life. She drummed her fingers on the steering wheel, realizing she'd just reached another crossroads.

As she sat pondering what to do, Willa Mae's words echoed in her thoughts. *"Don't cheat yourself out of happiness by not facing problems while they can still be solved."*

What if her friend was right? Could she have talked all of this out with Jake? Was she running away from the only man she could really love, and be loved by in return?

"You're what?" Desiree asked in disbelief.

Jake looked at Desiree and repeated the sentence. "I'm leaving the grounds and I don't know how long I'll be gone."

Desiree's mouth dropped open. "I don't believe it. In the four years I've worked here, you've never left the grounds while camp was in session. Except for supplies or a trip to the emergency room. What's going on?"

"It doesn't matter why I'm going. I called this meeting to ask the rest of you to cover for me until I get back. Now can you manage it?"

"Of course, we can manage," Ron said confidently.

"That depends. When will you be back?" Desiree quizzed.

"I'm not sure. It could take a day. Possibly two. I made up a duty roster and posted it on the bulletin board. If you have questions about your assignments, check with Ron. He's in charge while I'm away.''

Desiree turned to Mrs. Mullins. ''Somebody died. Jake would never leave Camp Wildwood otherwise.'' She turned back to face Jake. ''Aren't you going to tell us who died?''

Jake glared at Desiree. While she was a great waterfront director, she'd been somewhat shortchanged when it came to brains and tact. ''No one died, Desiree. At least not yet,'' he said pointedly.

She missed the irony. ''Hey, where's Hannah, anyway?'' Desiree asked. ''How come she doesn't have to help cover while you're gone?''

Jake ignored the question. ''I appreciate everyone's assistance,'' he told his staff. ''I'll make this up to you.'' Then he headed for the lodge parking lot.

Ron caught up with him outside. ''It's Hannah, isn't it? Aaron told me that she left. Are you going after her?''

Jake nodded. ''It makes no sense at all. I'm looking for a needle in a haystack. I have no idea where she's gone.'' He sighed. ''But I've got to find her.''

Ron reached over and grabbed Jake's shoulder. ''Sounds serious, pal. Are you in love with our Miss Hastings?''

''Yeah,'' Jake grumbled. ''For all the good it will do me.''

''Go find her. I'll keep an eye on Aaron while you're away.''

Jake shook Ron's hand. "Thanks, buddy."

With that, he hopped into the Bronco and headed for the highway. He had only one goal: to find Hannah and bring her back.

At the time Rachel left, he hadn't pursued her. Rachel had drifted so far from them that they could never be a family again. But neither did he have the burning desire, the all-consuming passion he now felt to find Hannah and bring her back.

So far he only had one hope of doing that. Willa Mae. He'd stop at the diner and pray that the proprietress had some idea of where Hannah had gone.

Even though he broke the speed limit, it seemed to take forever to reach the diner. He parked the Bronco and hurried inside. "Is Willa Mae here?" he asked a blond-haired waitress whose name tag read SANDY.

"Sorry. She's out for the evening."

Jake sank onto a bar stool and buried his face in his hands. His life was over. He'd acted like a jerk and let Hannah get away.

"Can I help you?"

"I'm afraid not. I need to talk to Willa Mae. I'm looking for a mutual friend."

"You mean Hannah Hastings?"

Jake jerked his head up and his heart started pounding. "How did you know that?"

Sandy shrugged. "I have a confession to make. I'm an eavesdropper. Willa Mae and Hannah had a long conversation a little while ago, and I . . . well, I lis-

tened in. You're Mr. Reynolds, from Camp Wildwood, aren't you?''

Hope suddenly flooded Jake's chest. ''That's right.
Listen, Sandy, do you know where Hannah is? I'd
appreciate any help you could—''

''I'm afraid she's gone.''

Jake's heart felt like it had dropped down an empty
elevator shaft. ''How long ago did she leave?''

''About half an hour.''

''Did she say where she was going?''

''She was considering two possibilities: going back
to camp to find you or driving to Kansas City. She
wasn't sure.''

''I see.''

Jake wasn't sure how much help these tips would
provide. But knowing that Hannah had considered
coming back gave him hope. ''So you don't know
which she decided on?''

''Actually, I do. I watched her. She drove to the
highway and flipped her blinker on to turn right.''

Jake's heart soared again. ''But I just came from
Camp Wildwood. I didn't pass Hannah on the
highway.''

''That's because she changed her mind and turned
left.'' The waitress shrugged. ''Listen, I'm really
sorry, Mr. Reynolds.''

''Don't be. You've been a great help.'' He slipped
Sandy a ten-dollar bill.

''What's this for? You didn't even have coffee.''

"It's for eavesdropping."

Jake hurried out to the Bronco and pointed it toward Kansas City.

Hannah turned the car radio on loud, hoping to drown out some of her confused thoughts. Should she have gone back to face Jake? Was she running away again?

Her wedding-day flight to Arkansas had generated problems for several people: for Paul, for her parents, and for the minister. And her flight from Camp Wildwood would probably cause both Jake and Aaron considerable pain. Was she behaving like a coward? Or would her leaving be the best choice for all three of them in the long run?

After driving about ten miles, she felt more and more lonely. Each mile that carried her farther away from Jake was like another dagger through her heart.

Finally, she could bear it no longer. She had to go back and face him. If there was the slightest chance they could work things out, she had to try. She flipped on her blinker light to turn into the rest area just ahead. But before she could reach it, a sound like a gunshot penetrated the noisy rock group on the radio and the Mustang started to swerve.

Had someone shot out her tire? She grasped the steering wheel tightly, fighting to maintain control, and was finally able to pull off onto the shoulder and bring the car to a jerky stop.

She rested her head on the steering wheel a moment,

trying to catch her breath. A blowout. It must have been a blowout. She knew her right rear tire needed replacing. Looked like she'd waited too long.

Hannah climbed shakily out of the car and went to survey the damage. The tire looked pathetic. Deflated, with a giant hole in the middle. Just the way she felt.

This stretch of road had little traffic. She certainly didn't want to spend the night here. She grabbed the jack out of the trunk and set to work. It was starting to get dark so she had to hurry. While she'd never actually changed a tire, she'd watched movies in driver's education class that explained the procedure. It couldn't be all that difficult. Heck, she'd taken thirty-five kids on a nature hike, run a square dance for them single-handedly, and cooked dinner for fifty people. A flat tire wasn't going to do her in.

Half an hour later, she'd finally gotten the car jacked up. She stood puffing a moment before retrieving the spare. Just as she went to get it out of the trunk, she heard a car pull onto the shoulder. Hopefully she wouldn't be mugged on Highway 71. She grabbed a hammer out of her trunk. At least she'd put up a good fight.

As she turned to face her attacker, she noticed that the car he drove was a Bronco. How ironic to be mugged by a man with a car just like Jake's. What a sorry ending to the sad tale of her life.

As the man got out and walked toward her, Hannah

peered into the fading light. "Do you need help?" he called.

Was she hallucinating? The man's voice even sounded like Jake's.

"No, thanks. I'm doing fine."

Hannah poised her hammer as the man approached. Suddenly, she saw that it really was Jake and her stomach performed a series of wild somersaults.

"What are you doing?" he asked.

"Changing a tire."

"With a hammer?"

Hannah realized she still clutched the hammer like a weapon and tossed it into the trunk. "Of course not. I'm using a jack."

"That's good."

"What are you doing here, Jake?"

"I might ask you the same question."

While he was only a few steps away, it seemed like light years. He looked handsome and strong and wonderful, and the realization that she loved Jacob Reynolds hit Hannah like the tsunami waves that follow a volcanic eruption. But she couldn't let him know that. "I decided to leave Camp Wildwood," she said quietly.

"Why?"

"I knew you weren't satisfied with my work. I tried to be a good activities director, but I never felt I met your expectations. And I also knew you didn't want me to get close to Aaron.'' She shrugged. ''Leaving seemed the best solution.''

Jake took a step closer. ''You ran away, Hannah.'' She could see the pain in his eyes now, almost feel it penetrate the night air.

''Maybe. But I was coming back.''

''Oh, sure.''

''I was. I intended to pull into that rest area just ahead and drive back to camp. But before I could reach it, my tire blew out.''

Jake walked up to Hannah and wiped a smudge of grease off her cheek. Then he tilted her chin up and looked so deeply into her eyes that she thought he could see straight into her soul. ''Do you know what your leaving did to me?''

His words held such a depth of feeling that Hannah's defenses weakened. She swallowed hard. ''I figured you'd be glad I left.''

''Well, you figured wrong. Oh, Hannah. Why didn't you come and talk to me first? We could have worked this out.'' He reached out to stroke her cheek, and the tender gesture sent a sensation of wonder sparking through Hannah.

She didn't dare give in to her emotions now. She must stay strong. But Jake's aftershave was working like an anesthetic, making her light-headed, drugging her so she could hardly think.

''That's wishful thinking. You and I want different things out of life.''

"What is it *you* want, Hannah?"

"Room. Room to breathe. Paul told me every move to make and it nearly drove me crazy. I intend to run my own life and make my own decisions."

"I want you to, Hannah. I'm no Paul Arnold. I'd never try to run your life. I can just barely manage my own."

"You mean that?"

"Of course, I mean it. I've watched you a lot this past week. And I can see from the way you work with kids that you're one terrific teacher. I want you to build your own career and pursue your own dreams."

"You do?"

"Of course, I do."

She took a steadying breath. It was beginning to make sense. Paul's way of relating to others was through domination, but not Jake's. He would give her room to breathe and the chance to grow. Leaving Paul had been the correct choice—he would have taken over her life. But she suddenly realized that leaving Jake was not.

"But that isn't our only problem," she said, still feeling confused. "You've made it difficult for me to relate to Aaron. Just when he and I were becoming friends, you told me to back off."

Jake sighed. "I want to apologize for that, Hannah. I've held Aaron too close. I know I interfered with your relationship with him. I just couldn't bear for him to get hurt again."

"I would never hurt Aaron."

A frown creased his brow. "It hurt him that you left."

"Jake, I can't play a role in Aaron's life that you don't want me to play. As much as I care for that child, I can't be part of his life without your cooperation."

He nodded. "I was wrong to overprotect him. But trusting again means taking risks. I wasn't ready to take those risks. Until now."

When he placed his hands on her shoulders, a series of tingling sensations zigzagged up and down her spine. "It wasn't until you left, Hannah, that I realized how much I love you."

"You love me?" Had Jake actually said those words?

"Yes, I love you." He pulled her against him, and his warmth and strength sent her pulse pounding.

He laid his cheek against her hair and sighed. It seemed the weight of the world escaped his body with that single sigh. "I knew I had to find you from wherever you had run off to and bring you back."

When Jake bent to kiss her cheek and forehead, the tenderness of his mouth against her face made Hannah's knees weaken. His warm breath caused the tiny hairs on the back of her neck to stand at attention.

"I love you, Hannah Hastings," Jake said quietly. "With all my heart." He tilted her chin with his finger and studied her face in the dimming light. "Do you love me? I have to know."

Miraculously, she found her voice. "I think I've loved you from the first moment I saw you."

He kissed her then, a long, slow kiss that alerted every nerve ending. The warmth of Jake's lips on hers made Hannah's senses swirl. As the kiss stretched on and on, she wondered how much more pure bliss she could endure. If Jake kept this up, she'd collapse. He'd have to call 911 to resuscitate her.

The aftershocks continued long after the kiss ended. She ran her fingers through Jake's thick black hair, then gently stroked his cheek. They had more to discuss but staying focused was proving quite a challenge. "So . . . so you don't mind that Aaron and I are friends?" she stammered, needing to know where she stood.

He kissed the tip of her nose. "If we can agree on certain terms, you and Aaron will be more than friends."

Uh-oh. He sounded like an attorney again. "Terms? What kind of terms?"

"I told you the other day that half of all marriages fail. If that's true, half of them must succeed."

"That sounds logical." But Hannah felt so starry eyed she wouldn't recognize logic if it came up and bit her.

"I have a proposition to make. But is there anything else we need to discuss first?"

"I don't think so. But I'm not thinking clearly. You're leading the witness."

His laugh was low and warm. "Attorneys are known for that. And we're also famous for being direct. Will you marry me, Hannah?"

She grabbed Jake's shoulder for support as his question knocked the little bit of breath she still had right out of her. "What did you say?"

"I just proposed. I'd like to join the successful half of the married population."

"You mean that?"

"Of course. Here. Let's make this official." Jake knelt on the shoulder of the road and glanced up at her. The love she saw reflected in his deep brown eyes warmed her down to her toes. "Hannah, I'm asking for your hand in marriage."

Suddenly all her doubts vanished. Hannah knew this was the love of a lifetime. "Oh, yes, Jake," she said happily. "Of course, I'll marry you."

He got to his feet and the huge grin that lit his face made Hannah positively melt. When Jake kissed her again, she wholeheartedly returned the kiss, melting into his arms. Finally, they pulled apart.

"This isn't the most romantic spot for a proposal," he said as a semi whizzed by. "Let me finish changing the tire, then we'll head back to camp." Jake walked over and peered into the Mustang's trunk. "Hannah? Where's the spare?"

A jarring recognition flashed into her thoughts. "Uh-oh."

"What do you mean, uh-oh?"

"It's at Bill's Service Station in Kansas City. I never picked it up after I had it repaired the last time."

He shook his head. "Never mind, honey. We'll send a tow truck out in the morning. Let's get back to the campgrounds so we can tell Aaron the good news. He's going to be one happy little kid."

Jake and Hannah climbed into the Bronco and started back to Camp Wildwood. When they arrived, they hurried down the hill toward the boys' cabin— to find little boy who knew they belonged together.

Epilogue

"**Y**ou look beautiful," Willa Mae said as she adjusted Hannah's veil. "The way a bride ought to look on her wedding day."

Hannah squeezed her friend's hand. "I'm so glad you agreed to be my matron of honor."

The older woman smiled. "I wouldn't have missed this for the world."

The screen door banged shut and Harold entered the lodge. His gaze took Hannah in from the tip of her seed-pearl tiara to the hem of her satin gown. He whistled his appreciation. "The captain's one lucky man."

Hannah kissed his cheek. "Thanks, Harold."

"You ready, hon?"

She took a deep breath. "Yes, I'm ready. Let's go." Hannah gripped Harold's arm, glad to have the older man to lean on. While she'd been hurt by her parents refusal to attend the ceremony, Harold and Willa Mae helped fill the empty spaces in her heart.

"Don't forget your flowers." Willa Mae handed her the elegant bouquet of gardenias Jake had ordered from a local florist. He'd said the wedding wouldn't be complete unless Hannah carried gardenias.

They headed for the campfire site where blankets had been arranged in two sections with a center aisle in-between. The tape recorder rested on a chair under a huge sycamore tree. Hannah smiled, realizing she'd learned to identify a number of trees and wildflowers on her Camp Wildwood adventure.

"Wait a minute, honey! We're coming!"

At the sound of the familiar voice, Hannah's heart started to pound. She turned to see her parents hurrying toward the campfire site.

"I'm so glad you're here," she said, embracing first her mother, then her father. "Now the wedding will be perfect."

As her mother went to sit on one of the blankets, Harold graciously stepped aside to let Hannah's father give her away.

Three men waited beside the charred remains of last night's campfire. The first, a minister they'd found listed in the yellow pages; the second, Ronald Sutton who would serve as Jake's best man; and finally, the groom himself.

One look at Jake took Hannah's breath away. He

was positively stunning in a ruffled ecru shirt and a black tuxedo. She could scarcely fathom that the tall, muscular camp director—who'd both excited and upset her from the first moment she stepped onto camp property—would soon be her husband.

Aaron and Lindy, the ring bearer and flower girl, hurried toward them. Dressed in a tux identical to Jake's, Aaron was a miniature version of his father. Lindy wore a frilly pink pinafore and the plaster cast on her arm was covered with autographs. Hannah and Jake's signatures were encased in a big red heart.

The minister welcomed the guests and when he nodded, Harold turned on the tape recorder. Organ music blared into the afternoon sunshine and the campers giggled in anticipation. Aaron offered Lindy his arm, and the two children made their way through the colorful assortment of campfire blankets. Willa Mae, an especially proud matron of honor, followed.

Then Hannah nodded to her father and linked her hand through his arm. They moved forward to the lively rhythm of the music.

From the moment she started moving toward her future husband, all Hannah could see was Jacob Reynolds. Everything else—every tree, every wildflower, and every camper gathered on the hillside—faded from existence. Only Jake remained. He stood proud and tall, anticipating her coming. A slight flush colored his tanned face and his dark eyes sparkled with excitement.

Hannah felt that all her life she'd been progressing toward this moment in time. Jake was waiting for her and soon they would begin their new life together.

"Who gives this woman in marriage?" the minister asked.

Her father cleared his throat. "Her mother and I."

After a brief talk, the minister asked them to exchange rings, then join hands. "Do you, Jacob Reynolds, take this woman to be your lawfully wedded wife?"

The question hung over the scented June air. As Hannah gazed at Jake, his dark brown eyes seemed to penetrate her very soul.

"I do," he said huskily.

"And do you, Hannah Hastings, take this man to be your lawfully wedded husband?"

"Oh, yes," she said dreamily.

Jake bent to whisper in her ear. "You're supposed to say 'I do,' Hannah."

"I do," she amended. "I most certainly do."

The minister smiled. "With the authority vested in me by the state of Arkansas, I now pronounce you husband and wife. Mr. Reynolds, you may kiss your bride."

He didn't have to say that twice. As Hannah's brand new husband gathered her into his arms, the scent of his aftershave mingled with the sweet smell of gardenias and left Hannah feeling light-headed. She felt more excited than she'd ever felt in her life. When

Jake's irresistible mouth touched hers, she slipped her arms around his neck and lost herself in the wonder of her husband's kiss. The children giggling in the background seemed a perfect accompaniment to this magic moment.

"Mr. Reynolds loves Miss Hastings. Kissy, kissy," shouted one enthusiastic camper.

A young voice broke through the dreamy fog that surrounded Hannah. "That's enough, Dad. It's my turn now. I married her too, you know."

Jake chuckled and stepped back as Aaron stood on tiptoe to kiss Hannah's cheek. "Miss Hastings?" he whispered after being granted his wish. "Can I ask you a question?"

"Of course, Aaron."

"Would it be all right if I call you Mom?"

Pride and happiness flooded Hannah at his sweet request. "I'd love that," she told her new little son.

The minister cleared his throat. "It is my distinct privilege to introduce the newlyweds: Mr. and Mrs. Jacob Aaron Reynolds."

Harold turned on the music as Jake and Hannah made their triumphal march through the colorful fanfare of campfire blankets. Shrieks of delight, and an explosion of birdseed tossed by the excited campers peppered the sultry air.

Jake's Bronco, heavily adorned with crepe paper streamers, waited on the hillside. Colorful tin cans hung from the back bumper. Jake opened the door and helped her in.

"Hannah Reynolds," he said proudly. "How does that sound to you?"

She smiled. "Like heaven just waiting to happen."